Peach Coloured Daisies

A Cursed by the Gods Story

By

C. A. King

Cover Design: Just Write Creations

Editor: J.D. Cunegan

This book is dedicated to readers everywhere. Without you,
my novels would be nothing more than words on a blank page.

-and-

To the people who have never given up on me, even in the rough times!

Look for other Books by C.A. King including:

The Portal Prophecies:
Book I - A Keeper's Destiny
Book II - A Halloween's Curse
Book III - Frost Bitten
Book IV - Sleeping Sands
Book V - Deadly Perceptions
Book VI - Finding Balance

Tomoiya's Story:

Book I: Escape to Darkness
Book II: Collecting Tears

Surviving the Sins:

Book I: Answering the Call
Book II: Pride
Book III: Lust

When Leaves Fall: A Different Point of View Story

Flower Shields: A Four Horsemen Novel

Drawing Strength From Words: A Four Horsemen Novel

Miracles Not Included

Twisted Tales of A Dead End Street
Shot Through The Heart: A Faerie Tale

This book is a work of fiction. Any historical references, real places. real events, or real persons names and/or persona are used fictitiously. All other events, places, names and happenings are from the author's imagination and any similarities, whatsoever, with events both past and present, or persons living or dead, are purely coincidental.

Cover Design: Just Write Creations

Second Printing: March 2018
Third Printing: July 2018
Fourth Printing June 2019

ISBN: 978-1-988301-21-1

Kings Toe Publishing
kingstoepublishing@gmail.com
Burlington, Ontario. Canada

Chapter One

A single tear, once released, opened the gate to hundreds more. Daisy couldn't have moved a muscle even if she wanted to - her body refused. She'd tensed up far too much waiting for the service to begin. A large black umbrella formed a canopy over her head, but it couldn't protect her from a soaking of her own emotions. A steady stream freely cascaded down her cheeks, following the same path as the first tears that had fallen. She made no effort to wipe them away.

Through blurred vision, she watched Father McGee do his best to perform a proper ceremony. A second man of the cloth held a similar umbrella to her own over the elderly priest's head. Having only seen him a few times before, his name eluded her memory. It was, however, apparent that this new priest was the one chosen to take over for Father McGee when the time came.

Daisy herself wasn't religious, but her grandmother had been. Every Sunday, they both dressed in their best outfits and scurried off to sit uncomfortably on hard wood benches for hours. While, after each service, her grandmother took away inspiration that only a God could provide, Daisy only heard empty words and promises of a better life.

The first weekend of spring was only a few days away. Today would have been their shopping day. Money had always been tight. Even though they couldn't afford a new Sunday best every year, her Gran made sure they both had a new spring bonnet to spruce things up. It was a simple joy, from a time long past - a tradition Daisy could have done without.

Daisy bit her lip and tasted regret. She hated hats. This was the first year she had taken it upon herself to complain. What was worse, she knew how happy it made her grandmother. Even with a life as hard as it had been for them, the woman never grumbled. How much had her gran given up raising her? How selfish was it to begrudge an old woman the one thing that brought her happiness?

Daisy released the air she had been holding deep within her lungs. The only family she had was gone. The funeral itself reflected how alone she was. There were no flowers or wreaths surrounding the plain wooden casket. Nor were there well-wishers or mourners. There definitely would be no fancy sandwiches with the crust cut off afterwards.

Daisy's grandmother, Sophie, had lived to a good age. Most of her friends had already passed on or were in no condition to attend an outdoor funeral, especially in the rain. There were no immediate family members to contact and, with all the weekly visits to the church, the only members of the congregation to attend were the two pastors. Daisy had no doubt that was more for the generous donation that was expected in return for their appearance. Of course, they would do a remembrance of the woman and her life at the service on the weekend. Everyone would comment about how sad Sophie's passing was. Afterwards, whispers of *which one was she* over afternoon tea and coffee would be the topic of choice.

Lightning cracked in the distance, issuing a warning that the weather was about to take a turn for the worse. A clashing of clouds shortly thereafter marked a possible distance - too close for comfort.

Father McGee took a step backwards, almost slipping on the mud. His protégé caught him with only a second to spare. That was her cue. She staggered forward. Her knuckles ached as they released their grip on a single flower. Daisy hadn't realized exactly how tightly she had been holding on to it. She felt the stiffness of the muscles in her hand begin to dissipate as the peach-coloured daisy floated down and landed on the casket. It rolled before settling on a spot where it would remain.

It was Sophie's favourite flower. She'd even gone so far as to name Daisy after it. Although truth be told, until now, she hated being called Daisy Peach. It was the sort of name kids in school made fun of. When one added in Daisy didn't have any parents to speak of, ridicule became her best friend throughout the lower grades.

She was older now - her twenty-first birthday was less than a week away. At that moment, standing in the cemetery, she would have given anything to hear her gran tell her story about running through fields of daisies one more time.

In her grandmother's version, and according to a family legend, any girl who found a wild peach-coloured daisy would find eternal happiness and marry their true love. It was a beautiful myth, but probably nothing more.

Daisy hadn't heard of any legend similar from anyone else. As much as she'd have loved to believe the story, she took it with a grain of salt, knowing it was probably a special tale made up just for her ears. Her grandmother always made her feel special - something no else ever had.

The crease on one side of her mouth curled upwards remembering all the times she asked Sophie why all women didn't visit a flower shop and buy happiness.

Oi! It doesn't work like that, Sophie would say. *A girl has to find it in a field of white daisies. That's what makes it special. Some choose to pick it - pluck it from existence. But why? If I ever found one, I'd let it grow and hope others would find their happiness as well. A cut flower, after all, will only wither and die.*

Daisy felt a lump forming in her throat - guilt. She had bought a cut flower and it was the only one present to honour her grandmother's life. Inevitably, it would wither and die like everything else in life, but she had sped the process up. She shifted her weight between her legs, wondering how she would feel if someone forced her life to end sooner than it was meant to. A strange feeling took form in the pit of her stomach. It had been an odd thought - one she was happy to have interrupted.

A throat-clearing noise from behind signalled it was time to go. She couldn't blame her two friends for not wanting to stay. The rain was falling faster by the minute and a cemetery is a gloomy place to spend an afternoon. Even the two priests had hurried away without so much as a goodbye - at least, not one she had noticed.

"Guess this is it," Daisy said, looking down at the flower. "I'll miss you." She bit down on her lip, swiftly turning to join her two friends and wondering where she'd go from there.

As it turned out, she didn't go far. Her two best friends dragged her across the street to a local pub, claiming they wanted to take shelter from the impending storm. Thankfully, there weren't a lot of loud University students drinking heavily and yelling obscene things at them. With the somber weather, the tavern was almost empty. Other than three guys sitting at the bar and two more playing pool, they had the place to themselves. She slid into the corner of a booth, hoping to stay hidden.

Daisy picked at the food her friends ordered. After only a nibble of each item on the taster's platter, she pushed it into the middle of the table. She sighed. In their own way, her friends wanted to be supportive, but neither understood the situation. How could they?

They both came from big families - wealthy ones, at that. She, on the other hand, knew the coming weeks would be filled with assessing assets against debts. In the end, there probably wouldn't be much left. There was even a good possibility she would be looking for a new place to live. The only real property her Gran owned was their house and that had a fair-sized mortgage on it.

Even without the financial woes, both of her friends had family to fall back on in hard times. Daisy wasn't as fortunate. Her mother had died during childbirth and her father high-tailed it out of town, not wanting the responsibility of a newborn baby. He didn't even know her name and she didn't know his. After her grandfather passed away five years ago, Sophie was her last living relative, at least that she knew of.

She certainly had no intentions of seeking out her father after all these years. Even if she did, she wouldn't know where to start. Sophie had never spoken of him and went so far as to fill in her birth certificate as *father unknown.*

"You should go see someone," Charissa suggested.

"You mean like a shrink?" Daisy asked, scrunching up her nose at the idea.

"Um, no," Charissa answered, winking at a guy sitting at the bar. She twirled a lock of her blonde hair around a finger. "More like a hypnosis specialist. You know - explore your past lives. I heard we re-live stuff over and over. It might help you."

"Right," Daisy replied, rolling her eyes. Past life regression was a little too far-fetched for her to take seriously. She wasn't even sure she believed in reincarnation.

"She doesn't need that," Jazz argued.

"Agreed," Daisy added.

"She needs a psychic," Jazz stated. "That way she can talk to her gran one more time and find out her future."

Daisy put her head on the table and banged it a few times. Unfortunately, it didn't make things any clearer - perhaps it even did the opposite. In the end, she decided maybe her friends were right. Even if she didn't believe in psychics or mediums, the idea of talking to Sophie one more time was enticing. It couldn't hurt. If the psychic was a fraud, she lost nothing and if, by some miracle, she was wrong about fortune tellers, she'd have a chance to say goodbye.

"Let's do it!" Daisy exclaimed.

"What?" Charissa asked, still ogling her new conquest. She had already worked enough of her magic to have the waitress set a round of drinks on their table, compliments of the men at the bar. One of them wiggled his eyebrows, motioning with his head to an empty seat beside him.

"Let's go see a psychic," Daisy explained.

"Now?" Charissa asked. She took a sip of the rye and cola that had been delivered. A quick smile and wave sealed the deal. She'd have a date on her arm before she left the bar.

"Why not?" Daisy argued.

"It doesn't work that way," Jazz explained. "We need an appointment."

"Really?" Daisy asked, her nose scrunching up like a bunny sniffing a carrot. Were psychics that busy that she needed an appointment to see one?

"You know," Charissa said, "a night with a cute guy could help you forget things."

"I don't need to forget things!" Daisy exclaimed.

“That's right,” Jazz added. “Besides, she only has eyes for a certain Professor.” She giggled.

Daisy sighed. How could she argue with that? It was true. There was one professor that she had been crushing on since she started at the University. She couldn't explain the attraction - other than the physical side to it.

The one thing she did know was she had spent most her life feeling like there was someone missing. When she was younger, she dismissed those feelings, believing it was natural for a girl with no parents. A few years ago, that changed. To some it may have seemed like a childish girl's fantasy, but Daisy knew in heart there was someone she was meant to be with. The professor happened to fit the bill perfectly.

Matt Demi, the University's expert on ancient religions, was, in her opinion, everything a man should be. He was smart, in good shape and drop-dead gorgeous. Her friends disagreed with her on the last part, but for Daisy, he pushed all the right buttons.

“I think I need to try and rest,” she lied. Being alone wasn't the top of her list of things to do that evening, but it was higher up than partying with people she didn't know.

“Are you sure?” Charissa asked, already halfway out of her chair to head towards the bar.

“Yeah,” Daisy answered with a meek smile. “You guys have fun.”

“I'll book the psychic for after class,” Jazz said, one hand carrying her glass and the other linking with her oversized purse. “Call me if you need anything.”

Daisy swallowed the bitterness left in her mouth from being ditched by the two people closest to her still living. There was grieving to do - stories to be remembered. They were supposed to be there to help her through.

She choked back tears. This time, if they fell, they wouldn't have been for her grandmother. These were pity tears. Daisy hated feeling sorry for herself, but a cold reality hit her. The dismal funeral she had just attended was exactly what hers would look like. She found herself daydreaming about who would bother to show up. Sadly, the cemetery in her mind was void of all people - except one. In the distance, she watched a figure coming closer to the hole that would contain her casket. It was Matt Demi, carrying a bouquet of peach-coloured daisies.

It took a few minutes before she found herself able to move. Her phone beeped as she pressed the numbers for the cab company to take her home - alone.

Chapter Two

Whoever said every woman should have a little black dress hadn't met Daisy. Black wasn't a colour that went well with her already pale skin and light ginger hair. The only thing it did match was her mood. It had taken her twice as long as usual to leave the house that morning. She lost count somewhere between the fifteen and twenty times she put her hair up and took it back down again before giving up entirely. She grabbed a black scrunchie and pulled every strand of hair she could find with one hand into a loosely tied ponytail, leaving a few straggler pieces framing her face.

She sighed. A nifty hairstyle was supposed to be the redeeming quality that helped others overlook the dark ensemble, not to mention the fact that she had opted out of wearing makeup for fear of crying. Running globs of mascara were more hideous than sporting none in the first place.

Even taking extra time, Daisy was still the first person in the lecture hall. Of course, she usually was and she liked it that way. The rhythm of the pitter-patter of her heart accelerated at the thought of the person who usually arrived after her - the professor.

Even though they had never spent any time talking about anything other than classwork, she felt a connection to him that was undeniable. She'd never admit it in public, but it was more of an obsession, really - one she tried her best to hide. She'd done a pretty good job too, until this year. Her lack of interest in men outside of the lecture hall made her friends curious. There had been little choice but to tell them how she felt. Of course, she kept the part about exactly how much she liked him to herself.

She inhaled deeply. The scent of woods and pine filled her senses. It was his scent. Her imagination worked overtime with the addition of the musky smell. She shifted positions, imagining he was there beside her.

“Good morning,” Matt said.

Heat rushed to her cheeks. The scent hadn't been part of her daydream. It was him. All attempts to control her racing heart failed miserably. How could she have made such a silly mistake?

“Are you alright?” he asked. “You look a tad flushed.”

“I'm feeling a bit off,” she lied. It was better he thought she had a touch of a fever than finding out he caught her lusting after him. He was, after all, her professor. There were rules about fraternizing between staff and students. Getting him fired wouldn't do anything for either of them.

“I can forward you the notes for the day through the school portal if you aren't feeling up to staying,” Matt offered. “It's no trouble.”

“I'm fine, but thank you for offering,” Daisy replied. “I was hoping to ask you about the assignment.”

“Shoot,” he said, resting against the front edge of the lecture hall desk.

A piece of chalk twirled between his fingers. Daisy mused at how he didn't need to look down to keep the white stick moving. She would have dropped it at least ten times trying to do the same. The professor seemed to possess everything she lacked. Together, they would fit perfectly, complimenting each other's strengths and making up for the weaknesses.

“I know we were supposed to find a positive impact Gods have had in the world as we know it.” She bit her bottom lip.

Matt tossed the chalk onto the desk. “But?” he asked, his full attention focused on their conversation.

“But,” she continued, “I am of the opinion that they didn't have a positive effect.”

“Go on,” Matt suggested, running a hand through his messy hair. She loved the way his bangs fell right back in place - even if he could have used a trim.

“I,” she started. “I believe the opposite,” she blurted out. “I think mortals were nothing more than play things for the Gods. They used humans, tossed them away and blamed them for anything that went wrong. If something bad happened in a God's life, there was always a mortal to blame.”

“Where's your proof?” Matt asked. “You need to be able to back it up.”

“There are several documented instances. The story of Medusa is probably the most well-known. She was a beautiful woman. A God forced himself on her and his Goddess cursed her for being with him. Every man she glanced at after that turned to stone.”

“A rather crude summary, but correct,” Matt said, smiling. He brushed the hair from over his eyes one more time. “If you can come up with enough to write an entire paper on, by all means, go ahead. I'm happy to read all opinions. You'll need more than one or two examples, though.”

Daisy smiled at the combination of his playful grin and green eyes. The extra work wasn't appealing, but he was. She didn't much care for in-depth looks into specific God lives. Most of them she found rather repulsive. Truth be told, she signed up for that class specifically because of the professor. She still wasn't sure there was a God she found interesting enough to stick her face in a book for hours.

Then again... Matt Demi would have made a God worth studying. That thought alone was more than enough to distract her. There was no doubt her professor had continued talking about something, but she was too fixated on what he'd look like without a shirt and tie to know what it was. She was no artist, but, at that moment, she would have given anything to sculpt him in white stone, especially if he was modeling. An elbow gently poked her side, bringing her back to reality.

“I thought you weren't going to be naughty until after graduation,” Jazz whispered. “Is that drool?”

“We were discussing the assignment,” Daisy argued. “Nothing more.”

Jazz laughed. “Alright,” she conceded. “But I want to be the first to know if something does happen. I want details.”

“You'll be the third to know,” Daisy said. “Did you get the appointment?”

“Uh-huh,” Jazz answered. “Right after class today. We are going to see the Fabulous Frieda. I've heard she is the most accurate psychic in the area.”

“Who'd you hear that from?” Daisy questioned. Her friend's idea of inside information usually amounted to eavesdropping on people in the checkout lane of the local grocery store. When it came to the supernatural, Jazz was all ears.

“A guy handing out flyers.” Jazz admitted. “It was a clear sign. We needed a psychic and there was this guy, wearing a suit from a thrift store, standing on the corner. It's like he knew we needed help. He practically insisted I take the pamphlet. Then I look down and whoa... psychic information in my hand.”

“I'm not sure...”

“This was meant to be,” Jazz interrupted. “Trust me. Signs like this don't get any clearer. Someone is looking out for you.” She gasped. “It's probably your grandmother. I bet she's the one showing us the path to follow.”

“Okay,” Daisy replied. “I give...”

“Good,” Jazz answered, flipping her curly black hair behind her shoulder. Daisy recognized her friend's signature way of patting herself on the back for a job well done. “You'll be thanking me later. This is exactly what you need.”

“Do I have to do anything?” Daisy asked. “Fast or drink water?”

“It's not a medical procedure,” Jazz chuckled. “She's reading your future, not looking at your ovaries.”

"I just wondered," Daisy snapped back, rolling her eyes. "It's not like I've ever been to see one before."

"It'll be fine. Just relax. I've done this so many times at fairs and carnivals," Jazz stated. "Maybe she can shed some light on the professor for you while we're there. There is no harm in asking."

Daisy felt the heat rushing back to her cheeks. Love was a major question people went to psychics to find out about. Why hadn't she thought of that before? She sighed. Jazz may have been her best friend, but she still didn't want her to know how bad this crush was. There was no choice but to go through with the appointment now. It was booked. She'd have to clear her mind of everything except her grandmother before they went.

"Daisy?" the professor asked.

"Sorry?" She was sure her face had turned bright red this time. There was no way to pass this off as a fever.

"Perhaps you and Jazz would like to share your thoughts with the rest of the class?" he asked.

"No," Daisy answered. "I'm pretty sure we wouldn't."

The laughter from her answer was far better than the embarrassment she would have faced if she told the truth.

Chapter Three

The frosted glass pane in his office door vibrated slightly from the outside. He glanced up at a shadow he knew well, poised to knock again.

“Come in, Frank,” Matt yelled without looking up from the pile of reports he was grading. “There is no smoking on University grounds.”

Frank flicked the ashes from his cigar on the floor. “No one can see me but you.”

“Yes, and I can see you smoking a cigar,” Matt replied. “You know as well as I do that the mortal sense of smell is stronger than their sight. Someone will catch a whiff of that thing. With my luck, I'd be accused.”

Frank inhaled deeply one last time. He examined the burning tip of the cigar briefly before plunging it down on the palm of his own hand. His eyes shut, savouring the feeling of sizzling skin. The extinguished cigar disappeared into his pocket. His eyes widened, pulling the corners of his mouth up with them. It took only mere seconds for the burn mark to disappear completely.

"Cozy office you have here," Frank observed, turning his attention back to the professor. "A little ironic, though - you being an expert on Gods. Appropriate, I suppose since you do have the blood of one running through your veins. I have to ask, are you having financial troubles?"

Matt didn't look up from his work. "You know I have extensive property and enough wealth accumulated to not need a job. I know someone keeps track of that stuff."

"I take it she is a student here?" Frank asked.

"She is."

"Does she know?" Frank asked. "Have you told her?"

"No," Matt answered. "That conversation would be a bit awkward. Don't you think?"

"How so?"

"Think about it, Frank," he answered. "In this day and age, what would a young woman think if a man approached her claiming to be her eternal mate trying to break a curse on her that has existed for thousands of years? I'd be in a mental ward for life, or possibly jail. I'm not big on either option."

"I suppose not. It would be especially bad," Frank commented, "considering you are immortal."

"Why are you here Frank?" Matt asked, growing weary of the small talk. His red pen drew a large C on the top left corner of the paper in front of him. After a moment of silence, he added a minus sign beside it.

"It's been a long time," Frank stated, throwing a hat on the desk. It landed right where he meant it to - blocking just enough of the paperwork to claim the professor's attention.

Matt leaned back in his second-hand office chair, admitting defeat. "A thousand years, maybe two. So, don't leave me in the dark. What urgent mission brings you out this way?"

"A certain Goddess requested I check in on you," Frank explained, slicking back his black hair. "She wants to know if you think you've found a way to break the curse. So she sent me to find out."

Matt laughed. "I had almost given up hope," he replied. "However, the fact you are here asking makes me think there might be a way. I don't suppose you know how."

Frank sighed. “I don't,” he answered. “And if I did, I couldn't tell you. You know that.”

“What can you tell me?” Matt asked.

“Things are changing,” Frank explained after a few moments. “The big guy is pulling further out of this world. He's ordered no more interference in mortal affairs - that means no new curses. That doesn't help you or me much, since we are affected by curses already in place.”

“But?”

“But,” Frank continued, “if a curse in place is broken, it can't be recast. That's got the ladies bent out of shape. They haven't forgotten their husbands' infidelities. They don't want to let anyone off the hook.”

“Perhaps they should try blaming their husbands,” Matt blurted out. “Do you know why everything is changing?”

“This world is growing. The mortals are evolving and some are being born with gifts. No God wants to be dethroned by a mortal. Something their prophets have revealed has them afraid. Before you ask, I don't know what it is. They don't tell me that stuff, but I can see it in their eyes and hear it in their voices. They are afraid of something. It's not like they can go around killing the first-born boy of a generation anymore, either.”

“No, I suppose they can't,” Matt said, grinning. “Where does that leave us?”

“Right here,” Frank answered. “If they decide to leave, I doubt they will be taking the majority of our kind with them. The question is, will we be able to find a way to be released from their grasp?”

“And you're hoping I can find an answer for not just myself,” Matt said.

“You're the brightest of all the cursed. You are also the most passionate. If anyone can find a way out of a curse, it'll be you. The Goddess believes that as well, or she wouldn't have insisted on me checking up on you first. I'm not asking you to do anything. I'm just doing my job.”

“What does all this have to do with the affairs of angels and demons?” Matt asked.

“Don't shoot the messenger,” Frank said, shrugging his shoulders. “Remember, we are cursed too.”

“I'm well past wanting to be a hero,” Matt stated. “Perhaps a thousand years ago, you could have rallied me to save the likes of all the immortals. Now, however, the only one I want to save is the woman I love.”

“You read too much into words, my friend,” Frank said, putting his hat back on his head. He tipped it slightly. He pulled out the cigar, placing it between his lips.

“What are you going to tell her?” Matt asked.

“I cannot lie. That is part of my curse,” Frank explained, heading to the door. “I'll have to tell her you aren't any closer to breaking the curse than you were the last time I visited you.”

Matt chuckled to himself as he watched Frank wave over his head before his shadow disappeared. He cupped his chin, allowing his thumb and fingers to brush over his two-day-old stubble. Needing to shave was something he'd inherited from the mortal side of his lineage.

He flicked the light on in the attached bathroom. Leaning over the sink, he turned the two faucets. A few splashes of water on his face was enough to get his focus back. He titled his head from side to side, examining the crude beginnings of a beard.

In the corner of his nose, a small white bulge stared back at him. Using his thumb and finger, he squeezed the clogged pore before it could tease him with its presence. He felt it release in a quick pop. The only reminder of its existence left behind was a few small splotches on the mirror.

It always amazed him how good something like that felt. He wasn't sure if it was a normal mortal reaction, or if it was his own response to being able to feel something human. These small moments were all he had to remind him he was different from his father. Gods didn't have zits to deal with. He didn't have their cruel nature. In his opinion, having a few blemishes and having to shave was a fair trade-off for having a soul.

Chapter Four

“Here we are,” Jazz said.

Daisy looked up at the three-story townhouse in front of them. “This is it?” she asked.

“What did you expect?”

“I don't know,” Daisy admitted. “Something a bit more out of this world, I guess.”

“Looks creepy enough to me,” Charissa complained, yawning. Of course, complaining could have been her middle name. She'd been born with her life already planned and handed to her on a silver platter. All she had to do was simply exist.

Jazz laughed. “Anything with less class than a five-star hotel is creepy to you.”

"Why did I have to come, anyways?" Charissa whined "I wanted to do hypnosis in a doctor's office, not play with a Ouija board." She was accustomed to having a doctor for everything, but drew the line at witch doctors.

"You are supporting Daisy. That's why," Jazz snapped.

"Fine," Charissa conceded, rolling her eyes. "I hope you appreciate this, Daisy. It goes against every fiber of my being."

"Do you even know what fibers make up your being, or is that yoga guru of yours picking them for you?" Jazz joked. "You better not start talking like him. I don't think I could deal."

Charissa replied by sticking out her tongue. That was her standard answer for any argument she knew she couldn't win.

"Maybe we should ring the bell," Daisy suggested. The door opened before she had a chance.

"Hello," a woman said. Her full-length multi-coloured skirt and frilly white shirt screamed of culture. The girls, however, had no clue which one it hailed from. "I am Maria. Come this way." Pieces of metal clanging together made an unusual song as she walked.

The inside of the home had a décor much different from the modern design of the outside. The hallway was dim - a result of the lack of light, accentuated by the dark maroon walls and tapestry-style runner hiding hardwood flooring.

Daisy stifled a cough, not wanting to insult the psychic reader. Shallow breaths were her only choice. The combination of stale air and dust made for an allergy sufferer's worst nightmare. She was relieved to see sheer white curtains flowing out from a light breeze in the room they were led to. The fresh air didn't last long. Maria untied two wine-coloured drapes made out of a heavy material. They fell down in place, blocking both the breeze and the sunlight from entering.

The rest of the room looked like a sideshow exhibit with a travelling circus. Built-in bookcases covered most of the walls - each shelf filled with an array of oddities. A semi-visible layer of dust meant few had been touched recently.

"Are those bones?" Charissa asked, gagging.

"Yes," Maria answered. "Of various animals, too. The far right are the human remains to which a cursed spirit was bound. Frieda managed to release the poor soul. The bones are reminder of the important work she does within the earthly realm. We are blessed that Frieda has such an amazing gift to share."

"I thought there were laws about having dead people in your house," Charissa whispered.

The ambiance of the room was set by candlelight. "I wouldn't worry about it," Daisy whispered back. "The stuff in here probably isn't real. That's why they keep it so dark."

"On the contrary," Maria argued. "Every item in here is authentic. Feel free to move closer and examine them, but I must warn you not to touch anything. As for the illumination of the room, Frieda is an albino. As such, she is very sensitive to brightness. Candlelight is much more comfortable for her to work in. I think you'll find it quite relaxing if you give it a try."

"These books," Daisy said, pointing to a shelf. "They aren't written in any language I know."

"English is Frieda's seventh language and, unfortunately, the one she is least confident in," Maria explained. "I'll be here to translate should the need arise. If you'll take a seat, we can begin." She pointed to a round wooden table in the middle of the room.

"Fifteen," Jazz whispered.

"Fifteen what?" Daisy asked.

"There are fifteen lace doilies in this room alone," Jazz replied.

"There are human remains on that shelf," Daisy complained. "And you are counting doilies?"

"They are a décor faux pas," Charissa stated. "I noticed them too. They really should have hired a decorator if they were planning to work out of their home. That's what I would do."

“Really?” Daisy asked, rolling her eyes. “I thought they went well with the shrunken head and African fertility dolls. I especially like the way that one looks on the child-sized coffin. Of course, I always found it in bad taste to keep fertility items near baby caskets myself.”

“Shush,” Jazz ordered. “Someone is coming.”

An older woman appeared, looking more like an apparition than the living. She wore a full-length red tunic with long sleeves. A similar coloured scarf covered her head. A chain in one hand attached to a gold ball the psychic swung back and forth. Smoke escaped through small slits cut into the sides. The strong scent of incense overtook the previously musty odour.

Jazz banged on the bottom of Charissa's chin to force her friend's mouth closed, but couldn't stop her from staring at the woman.

Daisy wasn't sure why any of them were surprised. Maria had, after all, told them the Fabulous Frieda was an albino. There was no need for them to gawk at her void-of-all-colour skin. The only strands of hair visible from under the scarf also lacked pigmentation, matching the woman's eyebrows. In fact, the only two things with colour on the woman at all, other than her outfit, were her red eyes and a single black hair growing out of an oversized mole on her chin.

A similar chiming noise accompanied Freida's footsteps. The movement of two women together created a new dimension to the music Maria alone had earlier produced. There was almost a practiced harmony to their movements. Frieda handed off the incense burner to her assistant before taking a seat at the far side of the table.

"Good day," Frieda said. "Who has the problem?"

"I do," Daisy replied. "It's not so much a problem as... my grandmother died and I want to make sure she is okay."

"Silence!" Frieda demanded. "I will read the cards." She held her hand out to the side. Maria scurried over with a velvet bag. After removing a deck of painted cards, she placed them in Frieda's hand. Maria backed away again, but not before bowing and thanking the psychic for sharing her abilities.

"Shuffle!" Frieda ordered. She closed her eyes and swayed back and forth in her seat.

Daisy's whole body shook as she took the cards from the wrinkled hands of their owner. A shiver ran up and down her spine before turning into a cold sweat. A card dropped by accident, falling face up on the table.

"Stop!" Frieda screamed.

Daisy obeyed. A lump formed in her throat as she glanced down into the blackened eyes of the Grim Reaper. It may have been only a picture, but she felt as if it was staring back at her. The card alone was enough to frighten her. "What does it mean?" she asked.

"Give!" Frieda ordered. She snatched the rest of the cards and laid them out in a cross formation. She stared past Daisy's shoulder. "Death walks with you."

All three girls shrieked and turned around, expecting to see something evil coming out of the walls. There was nothing. They glanced at each other and then back at the psychic.

"You cannot see," Frieda said. "But Death is always near you." She gasped. "You must break the curse! You must break the curse! You must break the curse!" Frieda stood and continued yelling the same line over and over until she collapsed in a pile on the floor.

Daisy felt as if the world was closing in on her. Her breath laboured. She needed air. There was only one choice - to run. She briefly looked back over her shoulder to see Charissa throwing money on the floor. After that, her two friends were in pursuit, following her lead. Her feet had a mind of their own, they propelled her forward, not wanting to stop.

She managed to catch a bus before it pulled away from the closest stop. Out the window, she saw her two friends with their arms in the air. Even if she couldn't read lips, she knew they were both uttering a few choice swear words for leaving them behind.

They'd be mad the next time she saw them. It didn't matter though. She knew neither of them would be much help when she was scared out of her wits. She needed someone she felt safe with; someone she could talk to. The only person who seemed to fit that description was Matt Demi.

Chapter Five

Matt sat staring at the pile of papers waiting to be graded on his desk. The page on top was already marked with tiny dots where the pencil he was holding had done nothing but bounce up and down for the last ten minutes. He tossed it aside. His eyes followed it as it rolled off the desk and onto the floor.

His thumb and middle finger pinched the bridge of his nose - a habit he'd formed over the years. Most of the time, he didn't even realized when he was doing it. Technically, it didn't add anything to the thought process, but he'd found it helped him to concentrate none-the-less. Today, however, nothing was helping.

Every time he tried to read one of his student's assignments, his mind wandered off - replaying his meeting with Frank earlier. It was entirely possible the visit was simply a ploy to crush his spirit. He'd get his hopes up, only to fail one more time. Gods, after all, had a cruel streak to them where the affairs of mortals and half-mortals were concerned.

Matt groaned, conceding defeat. He would take part in whatever game was afoot. The *what if* factor was too great to ignore. A win could put an end to the curse once and for all. A loss simply meant the game restarted again.

He knew better than to trust Frank completely. Any creature part angel and part demon was bound to have a few tricks up their sleeves. The question was, which side was Frank playing for and why? It didn't matter how many times their conversation replayed in his head, the answer simply wasn't clear - yet.

Matt marked a red letter B at the top of the paper in front of him without reading more than the first line. Placing it face-down in a pile of finished assignments, he moved on. Determined to concentrate properly on the next one, he picked up the paper next in the pile. His eyes focused on the name.

“Damn,” he whispered under his breath. It had to be hers. Out of over a hundred students, he ended up holding a paper belonging to the woman he didn't know how to save. He smiled at the way she wrote her name - *Daisy P.* with a flower doodled over the *i* where the dot should have been. Twenty-one was too young to die.

He glanced up at a rapping on the door. “Come in,” he said. With no scheduled appointments for the rest of the day, he was curious as to the nature of a second surprise visit. He'd instantly ruled out it being a return visit from Frank. He would have knocked much harder.

“Professor,” Daisy said, stumbling in. She grabbed the back of a chair to stop her tumble, pushing it forward slightly. The force was just enough to knock it on two legs. It crashed back down in place.

“Daisy,” Matt replied. “Are you okay?” He wasn't sure why he bothered asking. From the entrance she made, her trembling bottom lip and glossed-over eyes, he could tell she was a mess.

“I'm,” Daisy stuttered, “having a bad day. I really need someone to talk to.”

“Perhaps a grievance counselor?” Matt suggested.

“No, this isn't about my grandmother. Well, it began with her funeral,” Daisy explained. “I.” She paused for a moment, looking for the words to explain. “I'm frightened.”

“Is someone bothering you?” Matt asked, looking down the hallway before closing his office door.

“Not exactly,” Daisy said. “Actually, I'm not sure. I'm not sure of anything anymore.”

Matt handed her a bottle of water from a mini-fridge in one corner of the room. "Why don't you sit down and tell me what's going on?"

She nodded, but remained standing, using the back of the chair as a crutch. After a few sips of the water, she felt relaxed enough to speak. "I went to see a psychic."

Matt rested against the desk in front of her. "A psychic," he repeated.

"It was Jazz's idea," Daisy explained. "I wanted a chance to say goodbye to my grandmother."

"I take it you got something else instead," Matt commented.

She nodded. Her bottom lip protruded - a part pout that threaten to begin trembling.

"It's okay," Matt offered. "You are safe here. What did the psychic say?"

"She said Death walks beside me," Daisy blurted out. "I think that means I am going to die."

Matt cupped his chin with one hand, covering his mouth. He wanted to console her, but how could he lie? Her birthday was coming fast and if he didn't figure out how to save her, she'd be lost in the neverending cycle of reincarnation once again.

"Did she say anything else?" he asked.

“Something about being cursed,” Daisy replied, plopping down in the chair - her legs too shaky to be reliable even with extra support.

Matt squatted before her, taking her hands in his. “This is very important,” he stated. “I need to know what exactly she said.”

“Um,” Daisy mumbled. She searched for the exact words amidst a pounding ache that was creeping its way into her overstimulated mind.

“Take your time,” Matt offered.

“She said I have to break the curse.”

“You're sure?” Matt asked. “She said... break the curse.”

“Yeah,” Daisy answered. “I'm sure.”

“Did she say how?” Matt asked.

“No,” Daisy replied. “Do you think what she said could be true?” Her arms crossed her chest. “Do you know something about this?”

“Maybe,” Matt said, sinking in his seat behind the desk. “I need to pay a visit to this psychic. Can you write down her name and address for me?”

“I can do better than that,” Daisy offered. “I can take you there.”

Matt chuckled. “I think it's better if I go alone. You don't seem to be taking your first visit there very well.”

“I'm the one who the psychic is talking about,” Daisy argued. “I should be there. It's my life and I need to know what is going on.”

Matt sighed. He had always watched over her from a distance in the past. This time was different. Maybe that was the key to saving her.

“Let's go,” he conceded.

Chapter Six

“This is it,” Daisy announced.

“I don't suppose you'd agree to wait outside?” Matt asked.

Daisy's ponytail swayed back and forth with the movement of her head. “No way.”

“Alright,” Matt said. “But try to stay behind me.” He grasped the handle and turned. The door creaked open. The quicker they were in, the quicker they got out.

“Shouldn't we knock?” Daisy muttered.

“Shh.” Matt placed one finger in front of his lips. He'd never actually been a detective, but he had made sleuthing his hobby through a few generations. He'd even solved several high-profile cases. Unfortunately, there was no one to tell without drawing attention to himself. His personal records were all well forged, but someone digging hard enough might have found an odd paper trail connected to his existence. Being immortal was becoming more and more difficult with the advances in technology.

Daisy tiptoed behind him, trying to follow his lead. For her that wasn't an easy task. Matt was much larger, but moved with stealth and confidence in silence. Daisy, on the other hand, was more like an animal tangled in wind chimes.

“You have returned,” Maria said, stepping out of a shadow as if she knew they were coming. “Frieda has been waiting.” She motioned for them to follow her to the main parlour.

The Fabulous Frieda sat waiting at the round table - cards laid out before her. A few tufts of pure white hair hung down from the scarf covering her head.

“You must accept our apology,” Maria offered. “As I explained earlier, Frieda's first language is not English. When she gets excited, she tends to blurt things out. The intention was never to frighten you. We are here to help.”

“I'm Matt Demi, a professor at the local University. I was hoping The Fabulous Frieda could shed some light on what she said to Daisy earlier. She is a bit shook up by the events and asked me to accompany her.”

“Of course,” Maria said. “An explanation is included in what your young friend already paid. A solution, however, is not and can be negotiated after you hear what Frieda has to say.”

Frieda's hand glided over top of the card formation laid before her. A humming between an assortment of foreign words was the only noise stopping the unnerving silence lurking in the background.

“I don't believe I've heard that language before,” Matt commented.

“Shh!” Maria demanded. “Frieda is about to speak.”

“I see a curse,” Frieda said with a thick accent that hadn't been present before. “A curse that must be broken.”

“What is this curse?” Matt asked, Daisy clinging to his arm like she had been glued there.

“A curse of death!” Frieda exclaimed. “It must be broken or she will not see her next birthday.”

Daisy gasped. “But my birthday is only a couple of days away,” she squealed.

“Yes,” Frieda agreed. “Death is lingering around you, waiting. The two of you can break it.”

“Can you tell us how?” Matt asked.

“A potion,” Frieda replied. “A potion to open your eyes to that which you cannot see. A potion is your only salvation.”

“A potion,” Matt echoed. “Where could I find such a thing?”

Frieda's body slumped over on the table. Her eyes rolled back so only the white parts remained visible. Her hand twitched where it lay covering the cards.

“Come,” Maria demanded. “Frieda has exhausted her energy in the reading. I will prepare the potion for you, but I must warn you of the cost.”

“How much?” Matt asked.

“One thousand,” Maria answered. “The ingredients are quite rare and expensive. Of course, if you think you can break the curse without our help...”

“I'm afraid I don't carry that much cash on me,” Matt explained.

“No problem,” Maria said, holding up a hand-held payment machine. “We take all cards for your convenience.”

After confirmation of payment, Maria disappeared into a backroom and returned with a vial of blue liquid. “There is enough potion in here to last three days. Drink only one-third at a time. Good luck and stay safe.” She directed them to the door.

Daisy inhaled deeply once outside, clearing her passages of the dust and stale air. “That was a lot of money,” Daisy said. “I'm not sure when I'll be able to pay you back.”

“Don't worry about it,” Matt replied, shoving the small bottle into his pocket.

“I'm just one of your students,” Daisy argued. “Why would you do all this for me?”

Matt brushed the hair off his forehead. His eyes revealed a sadness as they searched hers for even a shred of memory. Instead, he found only questions he wasn't sure how to answer.

“I am just one of your students, aren't I?” Daisy asked.

“It's complicated,” Matt mumbled. “Can we go somewhere private to talk?”

She hesitated briefly, pondering the correct answer. “We can go to my house,” she offered, deciding to trust him. She coughed. “Did you smell that?” she asked.

“Smell what?” Matt asked, taking her arm.

“Cigar,” Daisy answered. “I could have sworn I walked through a cloud of cigar smoke.”

“Probably, someone has a window open,” Matt answered. “How far is your place?”

“Not far,” she answered.

“Good,” Matt said. “I have a feeling you should stay out of sight tonight.”

Chapter Seven

Daisy unlocked the front door and flipped the light switch. Nothing happened. “Um... I forgot to drop off a deposit to the power company. I've lived here all my life, but since the utilities were in my grandmother's name, they want some security.” She wiped the sweat from her palms on her shirt behind her back.

“We have a bit of daylight,” Matt said. “We should gather flashlights and candles.”

Daisy nodded. “Why don't you have a seat?” she offered. “I'll grab what we have.”

Two flashlights with questionable batteries and about a dozen candles was all she could muster up. She stopped in the doorway. Through the window, she could see the sun beginning to set. The last of the natural light shimmered over his silhouette. She bit her bottom lip, fighting the desire to run into his arms.

Reality set in, and along with it, panic. He was there. The man she had wanted for so long was with her. He cared enough about her to want to help her. But why? She needed to make a choice. Which was more important: her desire to be with Matt Demi, or her desire for answers?

"Did you find any?" Matt asked, staring in her direction.

"Yes," she squeaked, red creeping into her cheeks. "This is all I have."

"Those should last through the night," he said, taking them from her.

"Professor," she started.

"Matt," he said, looking up at her from a seat on the couch. He had already begun preparing the candles in various holders he had collected from around the room. A playful grin crossed his lips.

"Matt," she said, "I feel like there is more going on here than I understand. I need to know the truth."

"I suppose you do," Matt replied. "Forgive me for putting off the discussion. I'm not sure if you'll be able to accept what I have to tell you."

"Given the subject matter is psychics and curses, I can understand your hesitation," Daisy stated. "I'm not sure if any of this is real at the moment. I keep feeling as if I am going to wake up anytime to find out this was all a dream."

"You dream about me often?" Matt joked.

The heat coming off Daisy's face could have melted ice. "That wasn't what I meant."

"I was kidding," Matt explained. "I thought a joke might clear some of the tension in the room. Apparently not. Why don't you have a seat? I'll do my best to explain."

Daisy nodded. She plopped down on the far side of the couch. Grabbing the closest throw cushion, she squeezed it tight in her arms. Her gut feeling insisted she could trust the man beside her unconditionally - common sense, however, screamed danger.

"Do you remember the talk we had about your assignment?" Matt asked. "In particular, the part about Medusa?"

Daisy nodded.

"That same scenario happened more than was recorded in books," Matt explained.

"There are more women who can change people into stone?" Daisy asked.

"Not so much into stone," Matt answered. "There are more who were cursed under similar circumstances."

“Why isn't there information about them?” Daisy asked.

“Because few people know about them,” Matt replied. He lit the final candles. “Take, for instance, the God of Fertility. After a year with his chosen mate, a goddess of incredible beauty, the two had failed to produce an heir. She blamed him. That, as you might imagine, didn't bode well for the God.”

“That would be a rough day at work,” Daisy said, snorting afterward

“Actually,” Matt said, “that's exactly what happened. He was belittled and shamed in front of the other Gods. That evening, after drinking himself beyond the ability for reasonable thought, he came to the mortal world. He took a woman against her will.”

“Just one?” Daisy asked. “I would have thought the God of Fertility would have needed a few.”

Matt hadn't considered the possibility that there were others out there in the same situation as himself. Thinking back to his conversation with Frank, it did make sense. Frank had said he was the first to be visited.

“It's possible,” Matt admitted. “This story, however, is only about one.” He didn't have the time to explore *what if* scenarios.

“Got it,” Daisy mumbled.

“The mortal woman was left with child. The God returned to his realm to sleep off the rest of the alcohol. He awoke to the news his Goddess was pregnant with their child as well.”

“Oops,” Daisy said.

“Yes,” Matt agreed. “Very much an oops. He decided to keep his infidelity a secret and it remained hidden from his mate for some time.”

“But,” Daisy said, “I'm guessing not forever.”

“No,” Matt replied. “The woman had a boy who developed abilities no mortal should have. The child's unusual strengths did not go unnoticed. The God's indiscretions came to light.”

“Of course,” Daisy said, “he blamed the mortal woman for his unfaithfulness.”

Matt smiled. “Of course,” he agreed. “The Goddess was enraged. The mortal woman ending up being put to death as punishment for adultery. The boy, however, had the blood of gods running through his veins and could not be eradicated. He would be a constant reminder of her husband's deceit. The Goddess grew bitter and from that, a curse was born.”

“Okay,” Daisy said. “We have found the curse part, however, I am not a part god male. Where do I fit in?”

"The Goddess couldn't curse a child with her husband's bloodline," Matt explained. "That would have been too dangerous. It could have backfired onto her own offspring. Instead, she cursed the illegitimate child's mate."

Daisy looked up from her pillow. "How?" she asked.

"He, an immortal, would be forced to watch the woman he loved die on her twenty-first birthday," Matt stated.

"So she died?" Daisy asked.

"Yes," Matt whispered. "Only to be reincarnated and die on her twenty-first birthday over and over, countless times. He, a demigod, has tried to save her, but always fails."

"A demigod," Daisy said. "Matt Demi." She paused. "You are the child from the story?"

Matt nodded.

"And I am the one cursed to die?"

Matt nodded again. "I swore off my father and his bloodline after my mother was murdered. I have essentially lived as a mortal, although I cannot die."

"So," Daisy said. "You are saying I am your mate?"

Matt sighed. “This is the part that I mentioned would be hard to explain - at least without you thinking I'm some sort of a pervert.”

Daisy pursed her lips together and shook her head. “No,” she said. “Why would I think a professor telling a student she is his destined mate would be something perverted?”

“That's what I was afraid of,” Matt replied, standing. “I don't want you to think of me that way. I have to try to save you, but I'll watch from a distance.”

“Wait!” Daisy exclaimed. “What happens if you save me? I mean if I don't die on my birthday.”

Matt shoved his hands in his pocket. “The curse would be broken, forever. You'd live out a normal life.”

“I don't know why,” Daisy admitted, “but I believe you.” She patted the couch beside her.

“Thank you,” Matt said, sitting.

She gazed into his green eyes. A wave of emotion and desire overcame logical thought. She leaned forward and softly pressed her lips against his. A tender kiss wasn't enough to satisfy either of them. Acknowledging his hunger was as great as her own, she opened her mouth to his. He accepted her offering and devoured her love.

Her lips swollen from kisses, she broke the embrace. Taking his hand, she led him to her bedroom. Knowing the man had waited thousands of years to be with her, she could only imagine how the rest of the night would unfold.

Chapter Eight

A sheepish grin greeted her eyes - a perfect first-thing-in-the-morning sight. She couldn't help but return one herself. Hair fell down over his perfect green eyes. Daisy brushed it back, her fingers playfully dancing over his several-day-old stubble on the way back down. It was rough to her soft skin, yet the sensation was too appealing to ignore.

As if sensing her thoughts, Matt embraced her, taking the opportunity to rub his chin against her neck. She squealed, laughing. For the first time, she was happy - genuinely happy and it was because of him.

“We can't spend the day in bed,” Matt said.

“Why not?” Daisy replied. “If I only have few days left, I think this is a pretty good way to spend it.”

The corners of Matt's mouth curled down. “I'd prefer to try to break the curse, rather than simply give in.”

“So,” Daisy said, cuddling. “Where do we start?”

Matt closed his arms around her. “No idea,” he answered. “I'm hoping the potion will give me some answers.”

She'd forgotten about Frieda and her remedy. “Maybe you shouldn't chance drinking it. It might be poisoned.”

Matt laughed. “That's exactly why I am the one who is going to drink it,” he explained. “I am the immortal one, after all.”

Daisy frowned and pushed away from him. “Even if you save me, I'll still grow old and die,” she said.

“I think we should work on one problem at a time,” Matt answered, rolling over to kiss her on the tip of her nose. “Let's make sure you can live a full life before we worry about old age.”

“I can't help it,” she pouted. “The thought of not remembering any of this - of not remembering you...”

“We'll figure it out,” Matt interrupted. “I promise. We'll have more time if we break the curse. Even if you are reincarnated again, you will always be my mate. I will wait for you.”

“What would happen if I died before my birthday? What would happen to the curse?”

"Technically, it would be broken," Matt admitted. "But that is a big if. It hasn't happened in thousands of lives."

"You could..."

"No," Matt snapped. "You cannot die at my hands or anyone else who has my bloodline."

"I thought the Goddess was responsible for my deaths," Daisy argued.

"A Goddess cursed you to die," Matt explained. "She doesn't do the killing herself. She has faithful servants who carry out the orders. To die at the hands of a god is to have your soul destroyed. There would be no reincarnation. When she took my mother's life, she was so enraged, she did the deed herself. Her soul was destroyed that day."

"I could take my own life," Daisy whispered.

"I am afraid not," Matt replied, shaking is head. "There are other beings that dwell among us. They are not gods, but have their own powers. Some regulate death."

"The Grim Reaper?"

"A good example," Matt replied. "They can stop a soul who has taken life for granted from returning again. It would be too great a risk to take."

"So we're stuck," Daisy mumbled.

“Perhaps,” Matt replied. “But things are different this time. I feel like we have a chance.” He clenched the vial from the psychic in one hand. Staring into Daisy's eyes, he removed the lid and gulped back one-third of its contents.

“Feel any different?” Daisy asked.

“Much,” Matt replied. “I have you by my side. I never thought in a million years that would happen.”

Chapter Nine

The park was unusually quiet, even for a weekday morning. The occasional mother pushing a stroller passed by the park bench they rested on, seeming to pick up speed in their presence. Couples taking leisurely walks changed direction, avoiding close proximity altogether.

"Is it just me?" Daisy asked.

"No," Matt replied, smiling. "I see it too, even the birds seem to be avoiding us."

"Do you think it's the curse?"

Matt stared down at his hands. He had, at first, thought the curse played a part in the odd behaviour, but the hairs standing up on the back of his neck and the chill running down his spine screamed otherwise. “No,” Matt finally answered. “I don't think we are alone.”

Daisy trembled. Thoughts of strange beings sent to assassinate her were overshadowed by a vision of death itself.

“Don't worry,” Matt offered, letting out a large breath of air. “There are still a couple of days before they will come for you. This is something else.” He stood.

Daisy was about to join him, but heeded his motion for her to remain still. She watched him stroll across the path to a tree barren of all signs of life.

*****

“You can see me?” a cloaked figure groaned.

“I can,” Matt answered, shoving his hands into his pockets. He stood beside the creature, rather than facing it.

“It took you long enough.”

“Sorry,” Matt said. “Perhaps you'd be good enough to enlighten me as to who you are.”

“I am Death,” the figure replied, letting a ghastly laugh escape along with the words. A hand void of skin emerged from inside one sleeve. “Care to shake?” it asked.

Matt looked at the bone, blood and muscle death offered. “I'm good, thanks,” he replied.

Death laughed. “Don't tell me you are squeamish about such things,” it said. “You have seen more death than most.”

“I have,” Matt agreed. “That doesn't mean I relish the thought of it.”

Death roared another laugh. “Tell me, how will you try to save her this time?”

“Did you come for her?” Matt asked.

“No,” Death answered. “We both know it isn't time yet. In fact, her time shouldn't be for many years. I am merely a spectator in what the Gods, if you call them that, have planned.”

“I take it you aren't a fan,” Matt said, smiling.

“Let's just say, I have a job to do and they mess up my work with their little curses,” it replied. “I really have no interest in them or what they do outside of that.”

“What can I do to stop them?” Matt asked.

"Stop the Gods?" Death replied. "I cannot answer that, but your eyes have been opened. Now that you can see, you can fight."

"Fight what?" Matt asked.

"Look around," Death ordered. "If you can see me, you can see them."

Matt surveyed the park. He gasped, realizing it hadn't been Daisy and himself that others were staying clear of, but rather a gathering of foul-looking creatures. Although they looked as if they could walk upright, they travelled on all four limbs using claws to climb and, in some instances, hang upside down from trees. Their pure black eyes stood out against the wrinkled, whitish-grey skin that barely covered their bones. Matt squinted, but couldn't make out any identifiable gender that a total lack of clothing should have revealed. Each was identical to the other in every way possible.

"What are they?" he blurted out.

"You don't know?" Death asked. "You met with one the other day. He came to your office."

"Angels or demons?"

"They are one in the same," Death explained. "Angels by the hands of the Gods become the very demons you see."

"Can they be killed?" Matt asked.

"Yes," Death answered. "But not by mortal means."

"How?"

"I am afraid I cannot give you that information," Death said. "You know the places. Visit them and seek the knowledge you need. If you hope to win, you need to embrace that which runs through your veins. Your human side has no business in this fight."

"How will I know..." Matt turned to find Death had vanished. The Grim Reaper's words, however, still echoed in his mind. He knew where he needed to go.

*****

"I want to go with you," Daisy argued.

Matt placed one hand on each side of her face before planting a kiss in the middle of her forehead. "You can't. This isn't a place for mortals." He took her hand, leading her out of the park and back towards her home.

"But what if something happens while you are gone?" Daisy pleaded.

“It won't,” Matt explained. “I'll be back long before it's time. You have to trust me.”

“I don't understand why you have to go,” Daisy complained. She bit her bottom lip, fighting the urge to pout. As far back as she could remember, she had always criticized those women who used pouting to force men to feel bad. Yet, here she was on the verge of doing exactly that.

“If there is a way to kill the creatures who come for you, I can save you,” Matt offered. “Only certain places hold the information I need.”

“What should I do while you are gone?” she asked.

“Pay your electric bill,” Matt said. “I'd like to be able to cook you dinner when this is over.” He pulled her in by the waist. His lips met hers. “I love you always.”

Tears threatened to fall from the corners of her eyes. “I love you too,” she blurted out, sniffling.

“I'll meet you at your place before the sun goes down on the eve of your birthday,” Matt promised. “Or sooner, if I can.”

Chapter Ten

A film crew with cameras rolling wasn't what Matt expected to find at the normally deserted location. He sighed, not knowing how long they would be staying. With time ticking, there was no choice but to attempt to sneak around them. If there was anything lucky about this situation, it was that evening had already taken a hold of this region and tonight, there was no moonlight. The extra darkness provided a bit of extra camouflage, making avoiding being noticed at least a little easier. He watched the group split up. Two people stayed outside and the rest of the group entered the centuries-old castle.

“Damn,” he muttered under his breath. That was going to complicate things further. He waited for the outside crew to settle in, monitoring their machines, before making a move.

Every step he placed was as secure as a professional chess player placing a piece on the board. If he was going to outwit this team of reporters, he needed to make sure no mistakes were made. That included avoiding stepping on a branch or rustling leaves. Attention wasn't something he needed or wanted.

It took much longer than he anticipated to reach the hidden entrance. He took in a deep breath and grasped the vine-like structure protruding from the exterior wall. He bit his bottom lip as the vine sent thorns slashing into his skin - a reminder that immortality doesn't mean a life without pain. The guardian of the entrance way accepted his blood offering, revealing an open doorway leading to a spiral stone staircase going in one direction - down.

The wall made a stone-on-stone grinding noise, closing behind him. He descended by the light of torches to the lair of the record keeper. Although, he knew where each hidden sanctuary was, he hadn't actually visited any before. This was as new to him as it would have been to any mortal.

“Stupid ghost hunting fools,” a small creature muttered along with a few choice swear words. He stopped for a moment to stare at the new company. “The world is changing!” he exclaimed. “And not for the better, if you asked me.” His large ears twitched as he spoke. “How are we supposed to stay hidden if mortals aren't afraid of ghosts anymore? Do you know?” He pointed a long bony finger in Matt's direction. “I reckon you don't. It used to be easy to stay off the radar. Now everyone wants to see a ghost. They want to study them. All this fancy equipment, and for what?" He closed one eye tight. "They'd run in fear if they knew half the truth about what is really out there."

"Sorry for your troubles," Matt offered.

The creature sighed, then blew his oversized nose into a tissue, making a wailing sound. The crew upstairs was sure to pick up that hideous noise as a message from the beyond. No doubt it would be captured on some form of equipment and offered as proof in the form of a weekly television show. "So what brings Matt Demi, son of a God, to this humble abode?"

"You know who I am?" Matt asked.

"Well, of course I know who you are. I wouldn't be doing much good working here if I didn't keep records, now would I? That includes records of you and other children born from the union of mortals and gods."

Matt wasn't sure he agreed with that logic, but he also wasn't about to add time on to his trip by arguing. "I'm afraid I am at a loss as I don't actually know your name."

"My name isn't easily said by mortal tongue. You can simply call me Lumpkin. No wise cracks. either - and no, I don't like it shortened to Lumpy. I swear everyone is a comedian nowadays."

"It's a pleasure to meet you. Lumpkin," Matt offered. "I take it you are the record keeper of this fine establishment."

"Well of course I'm not the record keeper," Lumpkin bellowed. "He is."

"Who is?" Matt asked.

"Oh my," Lumpkin said, a crooked smile covering half his face. "You can't see him. That is interesting." A pointed, purple tongue escaped his mouth, saturating his lips before disappearing again.

"If there is indeed someone else here, I suppose I can't," Matt admitted. "Is it important to be able to?"

"That's a stupid question if I ever did hear one," Lumpkin blurted out. "How are you planning to have a conversation if you can't see with whom you are conversing?"

"I hadn't thought of that," Matt answered, rubbing the back of his neck.

"That's obvious," Lumpkin replied. His long, uneven fingernails scratched his forehead. "Well, come along. We'll have to sort this out, one way or another."

Matt followed his new guide through a maze of shelves - each one packed full of dusty books, waiting to be needed. In the centre of the maze sat an extremely long table, capable of seating a minimum of fifty.

"Well... take a seat!" Lumpkin ordered.

"If you aren't the record keeper, might I ask who exactly you are?"

Lumpkin huffed. "His assistant, of course. You aren't the brightest burning candle in the room."

"I suppose not," Matt answered.

"Well, if I am going to help you, you need to tap into some of that god blood of yours," Lumpkin stated.

"I'm sorry," Matt said. "I'm not sure what you mean."

"Oh," Lumpkin groaned, showing off a few sharp-edged, yellow teeth. "It's beginning to make sense now. You have some daddy issues."

"Excuse me," Matt said. "I have never met the man and I don't care to."

"Exactly as I said," Lumpkin offered, nodding. "Daddy issues. You'll need to rectify that if you want your answers." Using a long, crooked finger and thumb, he flicked Matt directly between the eyes. A small red mark was left behind.

"Rectify it how?" Matt asked, rubbing his forehead.

"I can give you advice, but I doubt you'll follow it," Lumpkin explained. "Somehow, your kind never do."

"Still," Matt replied, "I'd like to hear it."

"Fine." Lumpkin stood on the table and leaned in towards Matt's face. He pulled down the bottom of the demigod's eyes to expose the red fleshy area. After a few groaning noises, the dwarf-sized creature let go and took a few steps back.

"You need to embrace the part of you that comes from your father's line," he said. "Your father is a bastard for how he acts. You were born one. They don't hold the same meaning. Accept that and things will be much clearer."

"I've sworn off my father's gifts," Matt explained. "His kind have done horrible things to those I care about."

"Yes, well I did say I'd give you advice you probably wouldn't take - now didn't I?" He plunked himself down on the table allowing his stubby legs to swing off the edge.

"That's the whole thing?" Matt asked. "Embrace the side of you that murders and curses mortals?"

"Aha!" Lumpkin exclaimed. "Right there is your problem. We don't choose our family and they don't choose us. I'm sure someone out there probably has that job, but that's another puzzle to life that will have to wait."

“What's your point?” Matt asked.

“My point is, you are not your father,” Lumpkin stated. “He may do horrid things with his power, but that doesn’t mean you have to with yours. You still have to admit that you are who you are partly because of him. Once you understand that accepting yourself isn't validating him, then you can truly begin to see.”

“Perhaps...”

“Good!” Lumpkin exclaimed, clapping his hands together. “Admitting you have a problem is always the first step.”

“What?” Matt complained, wondering if he was attending a supernatural intervention.

“Close your eyes and feel the god side of you,” Lumpkin ordered. “When you can feel it, open your eyes and look around.”

Matt wasn't sure what to make of the suggestion, but followed the instructions. The sides of his lips curled downwards when his eyes opened to nothing impressive. Turning from side to side, he examined the room. Just as he was about to give up, he noticed something move out of the corner of his eye.

“Curiosity killed the cat,” Matt mumbled.

“You're an immortal, I don't think you have much to worry about in here,” Lumpkin snapped.

“Right,” Matt said, heading towards the wall where he had seen movement.

As he came closer, a shadow outline on the wall appeared. At first, Matt thought it might have been a snake, but the silhouette grew as he followed the wall. It was in fact a tail - and a rather large one at that.

“Lumpkin,” Matt called out. “Is the record keeper... a dragon?” He didn't need an answer as he found himself face-to-face with the green-scaled snout of a fire-breathing beast. He stumbled backwards, falling on his backside.

The dragon's head moved closer, sniffing at Matt's clothes for a few minutes before returning unimpressed to a sleeping position.

“I knew you had it in you!” Lumpkin exclaimed. “Well done. You have made the first step.”

“What happens now?” Matt asked, still on the floor.

“You ask him permission to look at whatever it is you came here to find,” Lumpkin said. “You need permission to touch his hoard.”

“Hoard?” Matt questioned. “These are books, not treasure. I thought dragons liked gold.”

“There you go thinking like a mortal again,” Lumpkin replied shaking his head. “What is it you came here for? I'll tell you - knowledge. What is more valuable than knowledge? I'll tell you again - nothing. To a dragon there is nothing more valuable. Books are worth their weight in gold.”

“I see your point,” Matt said, standing. He brushed off his backside. “What name should I use?”

“Oh. No mortal can say his name and he doesn't like nicknames,” Lumpkin admitted, throwing his stubby arms in the air. “You can just address him as record keeper. I'd do it nicely, though. Dragons can be a bit touchy. Always a good idea to stay on their good side, if you know what I mean.”

Matt nodded. “Record Keeper, please accept my apology for disturbing you. I am here to ask permission to look for information about angels and demons. I would appreciate any help you can give me. ”

The dragon raised its head again, this time snorting hot air and a puff of smoke. He nodded at his assistant and returned to doing nothing.

Matt stood still long enough to allow the smoke to dissipate. He might have to explain the odour to Daisy when he returned, not wanting her to think he was out partying with a bunch of friends. That was going to be another interesting conversation. She was taking most of the supernatural talk well, but he had his doubts about how she'd react to hearing about a real live dragon. He wasn't completely sure how he felt about it - and he was staring directly at one.

He turned around in time to see Lumpkin toss a book, about the same size as his own body, onto the table. It landed with a thump - a cloud of dust floating away, ready to settle elsewhere.

“There you go,” Lumpkin said. “Everything we have on angels and demons in one volume. I'll be taking my break now.”

Matt walked over to the table, shaking his head. That was one big book. He opened it and flipped through a few pages, before slamming it shut again.

“Lumpkin!” he yelled.

No answer.

He followed the direction the assistant had taken, finding him sitting with his feet up, watching a screen while eating popcorn.

“Lumpkin,” Matt repeated.

“I told you, I am on break,” Lumpkin explained without looking away from the screen. “I need to see what these crafty mortals are up to. It won't be safe here for long.”

“They can't see you,” Matt argued.

"Be that as it may," Lumpkin retorted, "they can see the books. They find this place and they will be printing stories about the find of the century and trying to decipher the meanings of works they could never begin to understand. Not to mention, I'd have a very angry dragon to deal with. That isn't easy, either." He chomped down on another piece of popcorn. "I have no desire to have my ass barbequed."

"I can't read the book," Matt admitted.

"Huh," Lumpkin said, sucking a kernel from between two teeth. "You can't read angelic. Who knew?"

"I'm guessing you did," Matt muttered.

"I had my suspicions," Lumpkin replied. "I can't read the whole thing to you, but I can summarize some of it."

"Couldn't we have done that a few hours ago?" Matt asked.

"You didn't tell me what you wanted a few hours ago, now did you?" Lumpkin complained. "Do you want to hear this or not?"

"I do," Matt conceded

"Angels are a cursed race from another realm," Lumpkin started.

"Cursed by the same Gods we have here?" Matt asked.

“You catch on quick,” Lumpkin said. “They were a naive race who believed the Gods were what they claim to be. Angels not only worshiped the Gods, but pledged themselves as vessels to do their bidding. Generations passed and one day a young group of angels forgot to make the usual offerings in a timely manner. The Gods were enraged and cursed them to a life of servitude until their race learnt the meaning of the words *pledge and commitment*. Yadda, yadda, yadda, and thousands of years later, here they are.”

“That's slavery,” Matt commented.

“Neverending slavery,” Lumpkin continued. “I doubt the Gods will ever set them free.”

“And demons?” Matt asked.

“Angels in their pure form do messenger work. Those unlucky enough to be given harder tasks have to fight for their sanity. Years of doing the worst deeds imaginable and enduring unbelievable torture changed them into the demon forms you speak of. They are but a shell of the creature they once were.”

“Can they be killed?” Matt asked.

“They are not immortal, if that's what you mean,” Lumpkin replied. “However, they also cannot be killed by mortal weapons. There are stories of some forged long ago that were made specifically for that purpose.”

“Where can I find one?” Matt asked. “A weapon capable of killing a demon.”

Lumpkin turned away from his screen for the first time. “I don't know,” he admitted. “They were all hidden. You would have to follow legends of demon hunters to find out and those aren't in our records.”

“Mortal records,” he muttered. “Somewhere filled between vampires and werewolves, no doubt.”

Lumpkin snorted a laugh then turned back to watching the ghost hunters. “I should warn you of what you are doing. Every time you kill a demon, a new angel is forced to take its place. You are condemning that angel to a life of inconceivable pain. Once a demon, they cannot be turned back. They are a damned race.”

“Is there any other way?” Matt asked.

“Not that I have heard of,” Lumpkin admitted. “To stop them, you have to kill them. To kill them, they have to be replaced. It's a nasty cycle.”

“Then I have no choice,” Matt replied.

“We always have a choice,” Lumpkin said. “That is the one truth in this world. You'd do good to remember that.”

“It's not like I can kill the Gods and free the angels,” Matt blurted out.

"Never say never," Lumpkin replied, laughing.

Chapter Eleven

Matt almost tripped on his way to the door. Perhaps he should have left her some money to have the utilities put back on. That was, of course, an afterthought now. He knocked twice on the wooden door, wondering if a secret knock might have been a good idea.

The sound of shuffling inside meant someone was home. Out of the corner of one eye, he caught a glimpse of the curtain in the window moving. He chuckled under his breath.

“It's Matt,” he called out. “You can open the door.”

As if on cue, it flew open. There was no choice but to pick her up to move inside. Her arms were wrapped too tightly around his neck and she showed no signs of letting go any time soon. He kicked the door closed with his foot behind them.

“I missed you too,” he said. “Did something happen?”

Daisy shook her head, but didn't let go.

“I'm going to put you down now,” Matt stated. “I may need my neck back.”

She shook her head again, this time in jest. “Sorry,” she offered. “Knowing death is waiting for me has me a bit on edge. There is only one day left.”

“I'm aware,” Matt said, plopping down on the couch.

“What did you find out?” Daisy asked, taking the seat beside him.

“The good news,” Matt answered. “I found a way to deal with them. The bad news is I have to find special weapons and I have no clue where to look.”

“Special weapons?” Daisy echoed.

“I was told to follow the myths and legends about demon hunting to find the answer,” Matt explained, rolling his eyes.

“The church,” Daisy blurted out.

“What?”

“The church,” she repeated. “Almost all demon-hunting stories involve priests. You must have read some.”

“Daisy,” Matt said, taking her hand in his, “there are far too many churches in existence for me to search in one day.”

“I know that,” Daisy replied, pulling her hand away. “We could go to one and ask, though. Maybe talking to one priest could lead us in the right direction.”

“Do you have a church in mind?” Matt asked. He had his reservations about the idea, but without any other course of action to follow, there was little choice. It was, after all, a place to begin.

“We could start at the church I go to,” Daisy suggested.

“I thought you didn't have faith in gods,” Matt replied.

“I don't, really,” Daisy admitted. “My grandmother did. She insisted I go with her every week, to one particular church. Gran always said if I had a problem, Father McGee could help me with it - no matter what it was. I think this qualifies as a problem.”

“Yes,” Matt chuckled. “I suppose being hunted by demons is a problem. Alright, let's pay a visit to Father McGee first thing in the morning and hope your grandmother was as wise a woman as she sounds.”

Chapter Twelve

The sun had barely popped up on the horizon when they pulled into the church parking lot. Time was precious and every minute counted. Matt looked at the watch on his wrist. It didn't say what time it was, but rather offered a digital countdown to midnight. There was under eighteen hours left to locate the weapons. That didn't even allow time for thoughts about the morality of what he was going to be doing.

It wasn't killing a demon he had a problem with. He was positive in his soul that those creatures longed for release in theirs. Even in the afterworld they would feel the torment of the life they had been forced to lead. To be obliterated out of existence was their only salvation. It was the thought of the angel who would take the place of the demon he slayed that he found disturbing. By killing one, he was condemning the other to a tortured continuance.

He pulled the cap off of the psychic's potion and drank another third of it. A lack of unusual sights over the past few hours had started to make him wonder if the last dose might have worn off, leaving him blind to the supernatural again.

Matt glanced over the church as they walked up the front path - partly looking for demons and partly out of curiosity about the building itself. It was obvious from the architecture, the main structure that made up the church was several centuries old. Repairs and upgrades from the last fifty years made it difficult to make an exact dating. Even the two wooden doors leading in had been recently replaced, although in a design consistent with the overall time period. In this day and age, he had half-expected them to be locked. The door, however, swung open easily under his grip almost knocking him off balance.

Inside, the reception area consisted of a small foyer with open closets to the left and right - presumably to hang up coats in colder weather. A half-wall built out of wood on either side of an archway acted as a room divider. The open middle section was a bit bigger than a standard door. A red carpet extended down the centre of aisles of church pews to a few steps leading up to an altar. The room was ominously empty.

Stained glass windows painted with scenes from a holy book kept the house of worship dimly lit, blocking all direct sunlight. Although he admired the artistic creativity, he found some of the depictions disturbing. In any other non-religious setting, the same scenes of torture might have been condemned as grotesquely improper.

"Hello," Matt called out as they approached an organ at the front of the room.

"Sh," Daisy demanded. "You aren't supposed to yell in a house of worship."

He smiled, wondering how many times Daisy's grandmother had drilled that into her head when she was younger. "How are we supposed to find someone then?" he asked in a whisper.

"We go to the back office," Daisy explained, grabbing his hand to pull him along behind her.

Matt followed without resistance. For him, curiosity was always a big motivator. He hadn't thought of a church as a place to have an office. After brief consideration, he decided it made sense. Religious organizations did have to make bookings for weddings, funerals, baptisms and exorcisms. Wondering how often the last one happened, he concluded it must have been much rarer than the other ceremonies.

"I thought I heard someone."

"Father McGee!" Daisy exclaimed. "I was about to come find you. We were hoping to have a word with you in private."

The priest glanced over his shoulder at his assistant. “Of course,” he said. “I think I know exactly what you are here to see me about.” He shook Matt's hand. “You are?”

“Matt. Thank you so much for seeing us. I know this is an unusual hour for visitors. Time seems to have gotten the best of us due to recent circumstances.”

“It's no problem at all, my son,” Father McGee said. “Let's go into my office where we can be a bit more comfortable.” He clenched a cane in one hand, steadying himself as he walked. “It may come as no surprise to you, this may be my last official act. I'm glad it is for you. Your grandmother was a wonderful woman.”

“Thank you,” Daisy replied, taking a seat opposite the priest.

“It's because of Daisy's grandmother we decided to come to you,” Matt admitted, closing the door behind them.

The office was plain and outdated. It was obvious all the upgrades that had been made to the premises had been restricted to the more publicly-used areas. The red carpet beneath their feet was stained in places and had patches where the fibers it was made out of had simply worn thin. Even so, Matt could tell the room had seen its days of grandeur.

“Walnut?” Matt asked, his fingers gliding across the surface of the priest's desk. It had character, including some ring marks from cups that had been set down without coasters.

“Oak,” Father McGee replied. “One of the finest English made. It's been in my family for generations. I donated it to this church when I took over the parish.”

“A generous donation,” Matt stated.

“A priest has no need for worldly possessions,” Father McGee replied. “Shall we get down to business?” He motioned towards the empty seat beside Daisy.

Matt checked his watch. “That's probably a good idea,” he admitted. “You said you knew why we are here. I guess you know we need the help of the church?”

“Absolutely,” the priest replied. “I am happy to be of service. Do you know exactly what you are looking for?”

“No,” Matt answered. “I have never been a religious man, I am afraid. The explanations given to me about these sort of things have all been rather vague.”

“Not to worry,” Father McGee said. “I can help you with that. Do you know how many we are expecting?”

“I'm not sure,” Matt admitted. He hadn't actually thought about numbers. “I don't know if we can get an exact count.”

“I understand,” the priest agreed. “There are always those stragglers that show up to these things at the last minute.” He sighed. “No one ever takes them into account - although, it would be easier if they did. Better to over prepare is my motto.”

“Forgive me, Father,” Daisy interrupted, her hands fidgeting. “You seem very calm. Do you do this often?”

“Well,” Father McGee said. “It is part of the job. I've done hundreds myself.”

“You have no morality issues?” Matt asked.

“Goodness no,” the priest replied. “People from all walks of life come to our church for this very purpose. We welcome them all. The church is here to aid wherever we can.”

“I have to admit, after talking to you, I feel much better,” Daisy said. “I've been rather stressed out lately.”

“That is a completely normal reaction,” Father McGee replied. “I am happy to take some of the burden off of your shoulders. You two have enough to worry about. We'll get you enrolled in classes right away.”

“Classes?” Matt echoed. “We don't have time for classes.”

“I know it feels like that, my son,” the priest offered. “You'll do better if you take the classes. I am afraid I must insist. It is a church policy.”

"We only have until tomorrow," Matt explained.

Father McGee pulled the glasses off his face and dropped his pen. "No one can plan this in one day," he said.

"There isn't any choice," Matt replied. "Anytime after midnight, they could come."

"What on earth are you talking about?" Father McGee asked. "You have to give notice to book the church ahead of time."

Matt pinched the bridge of his nose, his teeth grinding. "What is it you think we are talking about?" he asked.

"Your wedding, of course," Father McGee answered.

"Of course," Matt said, throwing his arms in the air and letting them fall back down.

"Father," Daisy said. "We didn't come to you to get married. At least, not yet."

"Why the devil are you two here then?" Father McGee asked, his eyes alternating between the two.

"The devil is getting closer to the correct topic at least," Matt said. "Information about demons is what we were actually looking for."

"Demons?" The priest repeated, shaking his head. "You are looking for some type of exorcist, I take it?"

“Not exactly,” Matt said. “Just weapons used in demon hunting.”

Father McGee sat up from his previous slouch. His happy-go-lucky demeanor traded for a stern look of concern. “You're serious? What for?”

“It's a long story Father,” Matt explained. “The bottom line is I need them to protect Daisy. If I don't find them before midnight, she could die. We need your help.”

“Oddly enough, you are the second person in my lifetime to ask me that,” Father McGee said, a blank stare on his face. “The first one wanted to see them - she wanted to know they were here. That was your grandmother, Daisy. I always wondered why, but never asked.”

“My grandmother?” Daisy shrieked. “Why would she know about all this?”

“I'm not sure,” Father McGee answered. “You are related. She must have known something of this predicament you seemed to be involved in.”

“Why didn't she tell me?” Daisy muttered.

“Only she knows the answer to that,” the priest replied. “And given the circumstances, you may not ever know.”

“I admit it is an odd piece to the unfolding puzzle. Given our time constraints, however, we may need to figure that out after tomorrow,” Matt suggested.

Daisy nodded, returning her attention to Father McGee. “Will you help us?” she pleaded.

“The Lord works in mysterious ways,” The priest answered. “He brought your grandmother to this church, knowing it had some rare artifacts in the cellar. I don't know how she knew. It isn't common knowledge.” He darted a glance between the two. “Now he's brought you two into my office looking for help. I have to have faith God knows what he is doing, because I don't have a clue.” He sighed, tossing his glasses on the desk.

“We'll be out of your hair in no time,” Matt offered.

Father McGee laughed, running his hand through what little hair he had left. “I'll have Father Galen show you the way. Take what you need, but tell no one. The last thing the church needs is another scandal. I'd like to retire without being in the middle of one.”

Chapter Thirteen

Father Galen took his time descending the spiral staircase. Matt glanced at his watch. They had already lost a few crucial hours.

"Patience is a virtue," the young priest commented as if reading Matt's mind.

"Perhaps," Matt replied, "but time is of the essence. A life is at stake."

"If you are looking for weapons," Father Galen said, "more than one life is at stake." He turned around and handed Matt a lantern. "There is no electricity in the older areas of the church, especially underground. Only Father McGee and myself know about what's down here."

"Why keep it a secret?" Daisy asked.

Father Galen laughed. “The church doesn't like to be known as demon hunters. It is rather counter-productive to attendance. Some of those weapons are also reported as quite dangerous - especially to mortals. In the wrong hands, they could make a big mess. Of course, there are a limited number of hands they could be in.”

“What do you mean?” Matt asked.

“Father McGee didn't tell you?” the priest chuckled. “I suppose he wouldn't have.”

“Tell us what?” Daisy asked.

“Anyone who has tried to remove a weapon in the last few centuries has turned to dust,” Father Galen answered. “It is all recorded in scrolls and filled by dates. You'll see inside. If you take any of the records out, make sure you put them back in place again. We don't have office help around here.”

“Has it really been that long?” Daisy asked.

“You are the first ones to try to find the weapons in the modern age,” the priest replied.

“Wonderful,” Matt said. “I always wanted to be a religious Guinea Pig.”

“Father McGee knew about this?” Daisy inquired.

“Yes,” Father Galen answered. “As head of the church, he is in control of the scrolls. He hasn't had the faith to try to retrieve any of the weapons himself though.”

“And what about you?” Matt asked.

The priest laughed. “I have no desire to be turned to dust. I know my limitations and I am not a hero spoken of by holy prophets from the old ages. We are here.” He motioned in front of him. “You'll either find what you seek or your own demise behind that door.”

“Are you not coming?” Daisy asked.

“This is as far as I am willing to take you,” the priest answered.

“Thanks,” Matt said, pushing past him. He snatched an extra lantern from the priest's hand. “Are there traps?”

Father Galen pursed his lips together and shrugged his shoulders. “Not in the first room. That's as far as I have gone. Good luck. For what it's worth, I am hoping you make it back.”

“Thanks,” Daisy answered. “So am I.”

The door swung closed behind them, hitting Daisy. She propelled forward.

“Whoa,” Matt said, catching her. “You are going to need to be a bit careful in here. In fact, maybe you should stay put in this room. I can play detective on my own.”

“There is no way I am staying here alone!” Daisy yelled.

“We still have hours before you are supposed to die,” Matt argued.

“There are worse things than death that can happen in a creepy place like this,” Daisy stated.

He couldn't argue with her logic. Technically, she wasn't completely safe anywhere down there. It didn't help matters that the young priest had given him a peculiar feeling in the pit of his stomach. A sensation that had now wiggled its way up his body, becoming a lump in his throat. “Alright, but stay close,” Matt ordered.

The room they were in was similar to the library he had visited the previous day. It was probably an addition, set up only to house the scrolls of information. The actual weapons were hidden somewhere beyond the next threshold.

Matt sighed as he opened the door to reveal a set of stairs heading further down. A musty smell of moisture and dirt greeted him in a less than welcoming manner. That door had been sealed for some time, yearning for someone to come along to unleash that which had long since gone stale.

"Careful," Matt said, pointing to a crack in one of the steps. "Don't step anywhere I haven't tried out first. This place may have been untouched for centuries. Anything could crumble."

"This is crazy," Daisy mumbled. "It's like the plot for a cheesy romance novel. Average girl is cursed by the gods. A hot guy comes to the rescue. They end up wandering around dark tunnels on some quest."

"Hot guy, huh?" Matt said, laughing.

"Usually they get to go around the world, though," Daisy complained.

"Yeah?" Matt answered. "Then what happens?"

"He saves her," Daisy replied.

"That it?"

"They end in up in bed," Daisy answered. "A night of heated passion leads to true love. They live happily ever after."

"I like the ending," Matt chuckled.

"Me too," Daisy admitted. "I wish we could skip to that part. I never was a big action-adventure fan. Now, science fiction I could handle. See any spaceships lurking about?"

“Wait,” Matt said, ignoring her ramblings. He motioned for her to remain on the last step while he checked out a bit of the room.

“Well,” Daisy called out, unable to see where he had gone.

“There are five doors,” Matt said, returning. “They are all identical. My guess is we only get to pick one.”

“No markings at all?” Daisy asked. “How do we know which one to pick?”

“I think we have to have a bit of faith,” Matt answered. That, of course, wasn't either of their strong suits.

“You know,” Daisy started, “that makes sense, seeing as this place was built by those who could handle the weapons.”

“I was thinking the same thing,” Matt agreed. He kissed her on the nose. He knew what he needed to do - get in touch with his immortal side. The problem was he didn't know how to do it. That thought was more than enough cause for the sigh that escaped his lips. He counted each door. “Five. Where else do we see the number five in history? It would be something significant; something you couldn't help but notice, but rarely thought about.”

“The Olympic rings?” Daisy offered, thinking out loud.

“Yes!” Matt exclaimed. “You are brilliant. They represent the continents.”

"The timeline would be well after all this, though," Daisy argued. "The games are more recent history than the Gods we are talking about."

"Yes, but the Gods knew all the continents before mortals did," Matt explained. "They would have counted them in a similar manner. This would make sense, especially with the Americas lumped together as one. It would be Americas, Europe, Asia, Africa and Australia."

"And how does that help us?" Daisy asked.

"We take the second door," Matt replied. "Europe was where the majority of Gods made their home. If I am right, these weapons were created specifically in case a demonic uprising ever happened. This is the back-up plan of the Gods."

"And if you are wrong?"

"I'll turn to dust," Matt answered.

"I thought you were immortal," Daisy shrieked.

"Yeah," Matt said, examining the door for traps. "I always thought angels were too. I've learnt more in these past few days than in thousands of years." The door clicked open. Matt shrugged his shoulders. "It didn't blow up. I'd say we are doing well."

"Great," Daisy moaned, following him. "Is that a lake?" she asked. "I didn't bring a swimsuit."

Matt reached into his pocket, pulled out a penny and kissed it. “Lucky penny, don't fail me now. Make a wish,” he said, winking. The coin launched up in the air and landed in the middle of the lake. The surface bubbled and smoked as the penny dissolved.

“That's not water,” Daisy said.

“Nope,” Matt agreed. “Probably some type of acid. I think we'll take a pass on swimming. There must be a way across. Look for a switch or lever.”

“What about these?” Daisy asked, handing him three round rocks, each one about the size of a baseball.

Matt tossed one in the air and caught it again. “They must be for something, but what?” The three balls were too uniform in size, not to mention too smooth and perfectly round to be naturally occurring. They were there for a purpose, he just didn't know what it was.

“It might be like a carnival game,” Daisy suggested. “The ones where you have to knock things down.”

“Or,” Matt said, pacing, “the type where you hit a lever and it releases the liquid.”

“Except,” Daisy argued, “I don't see anything that it would be thrown at.”

"You wouldn't," Matt said. "That's our problem. This isn't about what a mortal can do or see. We keep forgetting this place was built to be accessed by the gods. They wouldn't have wanted anyone else sneaking their way in."

"I won't be much help in that department," Daisy muttered.

"Stand back," Matt ordered. "There is a pillar on the other side."

"You think that's it?"

"It looks out of place," Matt answered. "I just wish I'd taken a few pitching lessons. Here goes nothing." He reached back and lobbed a rock. "Damn."

"I guess you missed?" Daisy asked, squinting.

"Yeah. Two more tries." The second rock followed a similar path as the first, narrowly missing the target. "Wish me luck," Matt said, winding up.

"Good luck," Daisy replied. She covered her face, sneaking a glance through her fingers.

"Bam!" Matt yelled, watching the liquid begin to disappear. "I guess I should win you some prizes when this is all over."

"It's draining," Daisy commented.

“The thing I hit must have been a switch that basically pulled a plug,” Matt explained as they waited for the last of the acid to clear. “I'm going to carry you across.”

“Why?”

“The ground might still hold a bit of acid residue,” Matt explained. “You are more likely to be affected by it than I am.” Without waiting for approval, he tossed her over his shoulder.

“You could have chosen a better way to carry me,” Daisy complained, her head hanging upside down.

“I can move faster this way,” Matt replied, already on the other side. He set her down beside the mechanism the stone had hit. “Grab the balls. We might need them again.”

Matt stood, staring at a long corridor leading to a plain wooden door. “Hand me one,” he ordered.

“What's wrong?” Daisy asked.

“I don't know,” Matt answered. “It looks too easy.” The rock landed with a thud. For a moment, nothing happened.

“Guess it is safe,” Daisy said.

“Wait,” Matt demanded, his arm acting as a barricade, stopping her from passing.

The rock began to shake, jumping up and down on the spot where it landed. After a couple of seconds, the ground beneath it gave way. It disappeared. The floor returned.

“It's a trap door,” Matt explained. He shoved the two remaining rocks into his pockets, barely squeezing one on each side. He ignored the accompanying ripping noise.

“Nice balls,” Daisy snickered.

“Very funny,” Matt replied. “I'm going to have to carry you again. I can move fast enough to make it across.”

“I feel like there is a *but* involved in that statement,” Daisy said.

“There is,” Matt admitted. “I can move quickly, but the door on the other side is closed. If it is locked, we may have a problem. I doubt we'd make it back.”

“Great,” Daisy mumbled. “What do you think happens if we fall?”

“No clue,” Matt admitted. “I guess we'll find out if it happens.” Before she could complain, he tossed her over his shoulder and began the sprint. “Uh-oh.”

“What?” Daisy asked as the floor gave way. She screamed.

Matt loosened his hold on her, letting their bodies separate just enough that she landed on top of him. “You okay?” he asked.

“Yeah,” she groaned. “I think so.” She rolled off of him.

Matt stood, brushing the dirt off his clothes. “Where's the lanterns?” he asked.

Daisy kicked the ground with her shoe, her hands locked behind her back. “One we left in the first room. The other, I put it down to pick up the rocks,” she admitted.

“It's still up there, isn't it?” Matt asked, brushing his hair back. He held it off his face for a few seconds before letting it flop back down.

“Yeah,” Daisy replied. “Everything happened so fast...”

“It's okay,” Matt said. “This is going to take a bit longer, but we'll get through.”

Daisy nodded.

“Hold on to my shirt,” Matt ordered. “I don't want to get separated from you.” His eyes watered a complaint as he strained to make out various objects. He focused on his own hand first, then moved on to walls and possible structures to avoid tripping over.

Simply embracing his own immortality wasn't as easy as it sounded. It had been thousands of years since Matt last used his gifts, including superior vision. It had, after all, been those very gifts that led a jealous Goddess to his family. That meeting resulted in his mother's murder and the very curse he was fighting. His biological father stood by and did nothing through it all. It was at that moment that he swore off all he had inherited from his paternal line. He promised himself he would never be like the gods - heartless and cruel. He clung to his human nature, attempting to preserve his own morality.

When one existed through countless lives, one tended to see things a bit differently than others. He had seen his share of people struggle to be different from their lineage. Only a small percentage of them succeeded. Those who didn't, inevitably let themselves down by not removing all chance from the equation.

There was the woman who watched her grandfather smother his food in salt. She was there when he died from multiple heart attacks. Swearing off salt, she vowed to never be like him. In the end she died from the same cause - not from salt, but from obesity.

Then there was a boy named Jack. His father lost their home at the horse races, leaving the family hungry and lost. Jack swore he wouldn't gamble, but bought lottery tickets hoping to win big with money that should have been used for food for his own children.

Of course, he'd never forget the lady who didn't want to be a drug addict like her crackhead mother. She walked around with liquor stashed in her purse for a decade before ending up in a wheelchair. Even after being charged with drunk driving, she maintained the accident wasn't her fault.

So many faces - their stories all the same. How many times had he heard someone utter the words they would never grow up to be like their parents?

Matt inhaled deeply. Did using his god-like gifts mean he would lose his humanity? He glanced back, gazing into Daisy's eyes. She was perfect in every way. He had waited so long to be able to express his love for her. If he saved her - if he became the demigod he was born to be, would he still be able to love?

As if sensing his uneasiness, she gripped him around the midsection and squeezed encouragement back into his core. That was exactly what he needed. He knew he would always love her, nothing could change that.

His vision sharpened. It was still dim, but clear enough to find his way to the wall. They had traded one corridor for another. One hand followed the rough surface of the stone as they walked. His breath steadied at the sight of a door up ahead.

Chapter Fourteen

Torches around the room lit under their own power as the door swung open. Matt pulled Daisy beside him. This was the place they were looking for. He glanced around, taking in every detail. An ominous chill ran down his spine, plumping out small bumps on his skin.

“Don't touch anything,” Matt ordered.

“Are those...”

Matt stepped carefully around piles of dirt, neatly mounded at the base of open display boxes. “If what Galen said is true, those are the remains of some poor soul looking for treasure.”

“If it isn't true?” Daisy asked.

“Then,” Matt replied, squatting down to take a closer look, “they were put here on purpose to scare off any would-be thieves. Either way, it warrants caution. One thing is for sure, it brings new meaning to the words, *ashes to ashes, dust to dust.*” He removed his jacket and placed it on one of the weapon cases, the buttons clanging against the glass.

Daisy rolled her eyes, shaking her head. “That wasn't funny,” she complained. “Do you have a plan or are we here for comedy night?”

“Yes, I have something in mind.” Matt answered, smiling. “I'm going to pick up the weapons and put them inside my jacket to carry them out of here.”

“Are you immune?”

“No idea,” Matt answered, chuckling. “I guess I'm about to find out if being immortal is all it is cracked up to be.”

“Wait!” Daisy called out. She held her chest, her heart racing. The word had come too late.

“For the Gods,” Matt yelled, in jest, grasping a sword with both hands. The air swooshed around the blade as if it was being cut into with a force strong enough to make a mortal wound. “I could get used to this.”

“You idiot!” Daisy exclaimed. “You could have been disintegrated!”

“There was only a small chance of that,” Matt explained. “These were made by the Gods to kill, but not each other.” He began gathering other weapons.

“What's wrong with that one?” Daisy asked, pointing to a crossbow.

“It's too big,” Matt replied. “It's also a long-range weapon. Blades are going to be more useful for this fight. Swords, axes, throwing knives, daggers or anything I can use in close quarters are the best choices.” The jacket bulged in spots. The buttons he had done up threatened to pop off. “That should be enough.”

“I don't think you could carry any more,” Daisy muttered.

“Hey!” Matt said. “I heard that. I'm stronger than I look.” He fired off a wink in her direction. “Now, all we need to do is find a way out.”

“We can't go back the way we came?”

“We fell through the floor,” Matt answered. “Remember?”

“Right,” Daisy said.

“Stay there,” Matt ordered. His hands fumbled over the brick and rock surface of the walls, pushing every possible nook and cranny looking for a secret door. He paused at one particular section with the smallest scrape marks in one corner.

"Did you find something?" Daisy asked on her tip-toes, her neck straining to see.

"Maybe," Matt replied. "I want you to come here. Make sure you don't touch anything and be very careful where you place each step."

Daisy groaned, but obeyed his request. She pointed her toes, daintily placing them down in clear spots on the floor.

"You are doing good," Matt said. This was about as graceful as he had ever seen her in any life. There were approximately twenty steps between them. With a little encouragement, he hoped she would make it before her natural clumsiness kicked in.

Matt found himself breathing in time with every step. A part of him wished he had gone back and carried her across. As she approached, he opened his arms ready to catch her inevitable fall. As if on cue, she tripped on her last foot placement. She tumbled into him. He steadied her, before wiping the sweat from his brow.

"Almost," Daisy said.

Matt's lips pressed against her cool forehead. "You're safe," he whispered. "Stand behind me." His fingers traced the edges of the block. Palm first, he applied all of his power into a push. He leaned in closer, utilizing his weight and shoulder strength.

Stone scraped against stone. The noise was deafening, not because of the volume so much as the level of annoyance that accompanied the sound. He could only equate it to hearing nails on a chalkboard or someone rubbing two pieces of Styrofoam together - two noises he had made every attempt to avoid in his extended lifetime.

Matt continued to apply pressure, inching the block further in from the wall until it crashed down on the other side. He sucked in air like there was a shortage, before taking a step back.

“That was fun,” Matt said, rotating his shoulder. The movement made its way down his arm to his wrist. His hand shook off the last memories of the work it had accomplished, although his muscles weren't likely to forget or forgive anytime soon.

“What do you think is in there?” Daisy asked.

Matt chuckled under his breath. He had thought it was obvious. “The way out.”

“Through there?” Daisy shrieked, her voice cracking. “Are we going to fit?”

“Not at the same time,” Matt answered. “These bricks are quite large. Not as big as the ones used to build the pyramids, of course, but large enough for a person to wiggle across.” He poked his head through the opening.

“Well?” Daisy said.

"It's clear," Matt answered, "except for a few cobwebs. You need to go first." He wiped his hands against each other before offering one to her.

Daisy glared at him. "Why me?" she asked, accepting his help.

Matt sighed. "Because," he started, "I need you to go through and move out of the way. You'll see a light in the distance. Keep heading towards it. I'm betting that will lead you outside the church. It's an uphill climb, so pace yourself. I'll be tossing the weapons in next and then I'll be following. I don't want you anywhere near the weapons when they hit the ground. Understand?"

Daisy moaned. "Alright," she agreed. It took a few moments for her to squirm her way through the hole. "Ew! I thought you said a few cobwebs."

Chapter Fifteen

Matt tossed his jacket armoury onto the altar, the weapons inside clanging together. His arms reached for Daisy's midsection, pulling her close. He picked the remnants of cobwebs and dirt from her hair.

“You're a mess,” he whispered, leaning in for a kiss.

“That's why you wanted me to go first, wasn't it?” Daisy smirked. “You didn't want to get your pretty face dirty.”

Matt laughed. “How'd you know?” he joked.

“Well,” Father Galen said, clapping his hands. “Look at you two. I have to say, I'm impressed. I had my doubts I'd see you again. Tell me, how did you make it past the acid room? I never could figure that out.”

Matt pushed Daisy behind him and squared his stance to the priest. He glanced at the weapons - instincts urging him to lunge.

“You won't make it,” Father Galen advised. “Try if you want, but you'll have to let her go.”

“Who are you?” Matt asked.

“Hm,” Galen groaned. “I pegged you for smarter. This isn't personal, you know. I really don't have a choice in the matter.”

“Galen,” Matt muttered. “Of course. How'd I miss it?” He chuckled.

“Miss what?” Daisy asked.

“His name, Galen,” Matt explained. “The letters can be used to spell another word - angel. He's an angel.”

“I don't understand,” Daisy stated. “I thought angels were good.”

“They are,” Galen interrupted. “Or were, once upon a time, in a land that is no more than a fairy tale to us now. We were not unlike yourselves. We worshiped the Gods, believing they were the creators of all life; good and just. Our ancestors pledged service to them. One day, a young angel broke that pledge. The gods cursed our race to be their servants until we learned what it meant to fulfill duty.”

“Have you not learnt that?” Daisy asked.

“Not in the eyes of the gods,” the priest explained. “It is their ultimate discretion as to when to release us from the chains they wrapped around our necks.”

“So,” Matt offered. “They will never admit you have learned anything. They won't easily give up slaves. I feel your pain. You must know we are also cursed.”

“Ha!” The priest yelled. “You don't know the meaning of the word. We are tortured and twisted into demons by the very acts they have us commit. It takes centuries to make a demon, sometimes longer. Do you know how they sped up the process for the first ones?”

“No,” Matt admitted. “I don't.”

“They pretended their best servants were being freed. The Gods gave them homes here in this world and allowed them a certain amount of freedom. Many married and had families. The curse, however, was never actually lifted.”

“How cruel,” Daisy muttered.

“That was only the beginning,” the priest said. “One day, the Gods demanded their will be carried out. The angels were told to bring their families and present them as gifts to the gods - offerings to prove their loyalty. Of course, with the curse in place, the angels had no choice but to obey. Their spouses and children were subjected to abuse as the angels were forced to look on.

Those who survived the first wave were slotted for experimentation and cross-breeding with some of the most hideous races alive. The Gods wanted to see what offspring they could produce. They forced the angels to deliver their loved ones for and, in some cases participate in, torture, mutilation and death."

Daisy gasped.

"It took only a mere few years to turn them," the priest added. "That is why you will never find an angel mate with anyone of this world. We all fear what the gods would do if they found out a child had been created. Of course, we are still forced to mate with each other - expected to produce an everlasting supply of angelic servants."

"Why do they need more?" Daisy cried.

"Hasn't your demigod told you?" the priest asked. "Tsk Tsk. Naughty boy." He turned his attention to Daisy. "A demon slayed is lost forever. The gods replace the deceased with an innocent angel. To save you, hundreds of angels will begin the process of suffering for eternity."

"You forget to mention that the demons are begging for release. Their souls can never find peace from the deeds they were forced to commit. I am doing them a service," Matt argued. "Being slayed by even a part-god puts an end to the suffering forever."

“True enough, son of a God,” Galen replied. “But does that make it right that new souls should be forced to begin the same horrible journey? And for what? One woman who would be reincarnated anyways.”

Daisy tugged on Matt's shirt. He pushed her back behind him. “What is it you are being forced to do? Are you here to kill her?”

“No,” Galen answered. “That isn't my task. I'm here to retrieve those weapons. The Gods want them back. They were becoming a tad bit impatient with me about it, when you arrived. Thank you for packaging them so neatly. I was wondering how I'd transport them seeing as I cannot touch them.”

“What do the Gods want with them?” Matt asked.

“I'm not privy to that information,” Galen admitted. “But, if I had to guess, I'd say they want to keep them out of your hands.”

“The curse on me satisfies only one Goddess,” Matt said. “I doubt that is enough to warrant you being here. Why are they worried about this particular curse so much?”

Galen laughed. “I don't think it's that curse they are worried about,” he said. “I think the Gods place more faith in you than you do in yourself. Whatever the case, I am taking them with me.” He pulled out a gun from inside his robe. “You'd be best to step aside.”

“That can't kill me,” Matt said.

“No,” Galen admitted. “It can't.”

Matt glanced at his watch. “There are still hours before she is scheduled to die.”

The priest laughed. “There are things far worse than death,” he uttered. “I know where to hit her so she is paralyzed. Would you like to see her as a vegetable? Or perhaps I should take away your ability to walk. Oh, I know you'd heal eventually, but until then, you would be forced to lie there and watch the little lady die without being able to move a muscle to help her. Do you want that?”

“No,” Matt said, glancing over the priest's shoulder at the altar. “I'm not going to make a move.”

“Good,” Galen said.

“Neither are you!” Father McGee yelled. “My God is good, not like yours.” He grabbed a dagger from the pile and plunged it deep into Galen's side. Both men turned into neat piles of dust.

Daisy turned her head and cried. Each tear she shed had its own meaning, whether for a fallen angel or Father McGee.

“Sh,” Matt whispered, his hands running over her hair. “It's almost over. The sun will be going down soon. I need to prepare.”

Chapter Sixteen

“What's the plan?” Daisy asked, watching him work. “Can I help with something?”

“Yeah,” Matt answered without looking up. “We need to make your house a fortress in the next four hours. Grab anything made of wood that you don't mind me breaking.”

Daisy came back with a single wooden chair. “You can use this,” she offered.

“You're kidding, right?” Matt asked, shaking his head. He wasn't sure why he asked, he already knew the answer. “This is serious, Daisy. This is your life. Material things can be replaced. I'll buy you new furniture, if that is what you are worried about.”

“What about the angels?” Daisy asked. “Will we really be condemning them to a life of torture?”

Matt huffed out air, forcing his bangs to fly up and fall back down again. “I don't know,” he admitted. “I don't want to hurt them any more than you do. After this is over, I'll do my best to figure something out. Galen did say it takes hundreds of years to change them. If there is a way to save them, we'll find it.”

“Promise?” Daisy asked.

Matt stood and took her hands in his own. “Promise,” he whispered gently in her ear.

“Gods without compassion,” she whispered back. “How did we end up with those?”

“Anyone can proclaim themselves a God,” Matt answered, embracing her. “That doesn't mean they truly are. Father McGee was right. There must be a true God out there - one that loves and forgives. Maybe it is the God he worshiped.”

“How do you know there is one different from the others?” Daisy asked.

“Because,” Matt answered, “the ones we are dealing with are frightened. An omnipotent power shouldn't fear its own creations.” He brushed his lips against her cheek. “You have bookshelves in the other room. If you empty them, I can barricade the windows.”

“Will it make a difference?” Daisy asked. “They are demons, after all. I think they'll find a way in.”

Matt chuckled. “They most definitely are going to find a way in. That doesn't mean we have to make it easy for them. We need to last twenty-four hours. I'd like to make them waste a few getting to us.”

“Do you think they will attack right at midnight?”

“I don't know,” Matt answered. “We need to be prepared in case they do.”

She piled the books on the floor. A picture frame shook in her hands. She sniffled back her tears, the sight of her grandmother drawing out emotions she was too tired to control.

“I wish I had met her,” Matt commented. “The daisies she is holding remind me of your name.”

Daisy smiled. “You caught that, huh? She used to tell me this story. It was apparently my mom's favourite. That's why she named me after it. According to the tale, if a maiden walking through a field stumbles upon a peach-coloured daisy, it's good luck. She will marry her true love and the couple will be happy together through all eternity - wanting for nothing.”

“That's a beautiful story,” Matt said.

“It is,” Daisy replied. “I know it's all supposed to happen in a wild field, but I was going plant all peach-coloured daisies in the garden this year. It reminds me of family.” She placed the picture on top of the pile of books. “The shelves are ready.”

“Perfect,” Matt, said, breaking apart the first shelf. “When this is over, I am going to take you away and give you a garden full of any type of daisy you want.”

The windows were the last part of the house he needed to prepare. “We'll head to the basement after this,” Matt said, nailing the last piece of wood into place. “Double check I've locked and barricaded all the doors.”

“All done.” Daisy returned out of breath.

Matt's watch beeped. “It's time.” He pulled Daisy close. “Happy birthday. Sorry I didn't get you anything. Next year, we'll celebrate any way you want.”

Chapter Seventeen

It felt like an eternity, waiting around the basement for something to happen. It had been quiet all day - too quiet.

“Where are they?” Daisy asked.

“I don't know,” Matt replied. The truth was he was going over in his head all of the possible mistakes he had made. A demon needed only to set the house on fire and they were trapped. He wondered if their thought process was intact enough to think of such a plan.

Making them wait could also have been a plan. The effects of not sleeping were starting to show for both of them. He was counting on sheer adrenaline to see him through to midnight. He watched Daisy pace, biting her nails. The bags under her eyes told him she was on her last wind as well.

The basement décor didn't help the building's somber mood. It was dark, musty and dismal; the perfect breeding grounds for worry and doubt. He watched a spider skitter across the floor to find a hiding spot under a stack of boxes.

"They are coming," Matt announced, the hairs on his back alerting him as to the danger before any other sense could have known. He pulled the cap off of the potion and guzzled back the final mouthful.

"Are you sure?"

"Yes," Matt answered, looking at his watch. "We have to hold them off for two hours. That's doable. Better than twenty-two."

"Why do you think the waited so long?" Daisy asked.

"To wear us down," Matt explained. The lights flickered, then went out altogether. "Or for it to get dark. Remember what we practiced. Stay in the middle of the room and away from any blades." He stood, taking a stance facing the stairs. His eyes shifted from side to side. The spider had the right idea - it was nowhere to be seen.

A crash from upstairs meant the beasts had made short work of his barricades, probably only buying them ten minutes at the most. It was only a matter of time now before they found their way to the basement. A bead of sweat rolled off his nose, hitting the cement floor. The silence was broken.

A reflection in the blade he gripped tightly told him it was time. He sliced the first demon in half before he saw its whole body. There were more than Matt had anticipated. He cleared his mind, concentrating on only the sound of his own breathing and the blade. It swung wildly around, taking down another two.

Spinning backwards, he knocked one away from Daisy, then pinned it to the wall with his sword. It screeched in pain before going limp. Reaching down, he grabbed a series of throwing knives and hurled them, each making contact with its intended target.

The assault continued. At one point, he felt the sting of claws on the side of his face. A liquid trickled down his forehead. He wasn't sure if it was blood or sweat, or perhaps a combination of the two. His muscles ached, tiring under the pressure of the continued activity.

He glanced back at Daisy, cowering in a ball on the floor. This was his chance to free her - to free them both. That was the inspiration he needed to continue. Adrenaline kicked in and his movements quickened.

Their numbers increased. Several seized the opportunity to jump on Matt at once, their teeth and claws penetrating his skin. Each bite; each slice; was a moment of agonizing pain. He held back from howling in agony. He understood now why the Gods needed weapons. These demons could wound them. The realization he was faltering brought a new revelation to light. There was a good chance these demons could kill him. “Never say never,” he muttered, laughing at his own stupidity.

Daisy's screams in the background found his ears. He mustered every ounce of strength he could find, sending demons flying across the room in every direction. Even if he didn't survive this, he planned to make sure she did.

To his horror, one single demon was already headed for Daisy. It stalked around her. Matt lunged forward, hoping to land on it, but missed. It climbed on top of her, its gaping jaw open. There was nothing Matt could do. He reached out one hand towards her.

An alarm sounded. “It's over!” he yelled.

The creature hissed in retreat. The bodies of the lost demons disappeared. Matt gasped for air, rolling flat onto his back. They had won the battle. He chuckled. The laugh turned into a cough, accompanied by a trickling of blood. He looked down at a claw still stuck in his chest. Grasping the end, he pulled it out, groaning. It tumbled out of his open hand onto the cement floor before disappearing.

He felt Daisy take his hand. Tears splashed on his face. He reached up and wiped new ones away.

"Don't cry," he whispered. "I'm fine - just a little tired." He closed his eyes - the world went black.

Chapter Eighteen

Daisy walked up to the door and then away again. It seemed like another lifetime when she first walked into Fabulous Frieda's parlour to try to communicate with her grandmother. Now, here she was again, but for a different reason.

According to her watch, only five minutes had passed since she arrived. She tapped on the glass cover, wondering if it had stopped working. With the second hand still ticking away, it had to be right. But then why did it feel like it had been hours?

Air felt heavy in her lungs. She exhaled, taking a few steps towards the door again.

"Hey!"

She swiveled on the spot. "Hey."

“Sorry I'm late,” Matt said. “It took a little longer than expected to hand in my resignation.” He planted a firm kiss on her cheek. “You weren't thinking about going in without me, were you?”

“Actually, I thought you might already be inside,” Daisy admitted, accepting his offer to hold the door open.

Little had changed inside. Musty air greeted them in a less than inviting manner. Daisy plugged her nose, trying to avoid an inevitable round of sneezes.

“I'm surprised Maria didn't hear that,” Daisy said.

“I'm not,” Matt replied. “Someone is watching baseball. I doubt they heard you.”

“Baseball?” Daisy echoed. “I don't remember there being a television anywhere in here.”

The further down the corridor they went, the louder the game became. Standing in the parlour entrance, Daisy gasped. It wasn’t the large screen television mounted to the wall behind the bookshelves that surprised her. Although it could have been, if there wasn't something ten times more shocking.

There, in the middle of the room, Fabulous Frieda sat at the table - looking not so fabulous. Daisy alternated glances between a wig piled on the table beside an overflowing ashtray, a container of white makeup and the now-bald psychic.

If Frieda hadn't been wearing the same outfit as when they previously attended, Daisy wouldn't have recognized her - or him, she wasn't sure which. She gasped. Even the red eyes were now brown. She had been bamboozled in the worst possible way.

“Awe crap!” Frieda exclaimed, a cigarette dangling out of her mouth. “Don't you two know how to use a door bell?”

“Are you...”

“A man?” Frieda interrupted. “Yeah. I'm a man, so what?” He rubbed his bald head.

“Sorry,” Matt offered. “It was a bit of a surprise. I have to admit, you had us completely fooled.”

“Look,” Freida said. “We don't give refunds, if that's what you are looking for.” He flicked the ashes off his cigarette, missing the ashtray completely. “I could call the cops. You two are trespassing. There's laws against walking into a person's house uninvited.”

“Go ahead,” Matt replied. “Call the police.”

“If you are insinuating we are doing something illegal, you got it wrong,” Frieda said, pointing two fingers with his cigarette between them in their direction. “We do a legitimate service here.” He scratched his crotch with his free hand and adjusted his position.

“And what service is that?” Daisy asked.

“Damn,” Frieda said, shaking his head. “I knew you two were going to be trouble.” He clicked a remote control and the room went silent. “We give closure to people.”

“Closure?” Matt echoed.

“That's right,” Frieda said. “It helps people - most people. Lots of folks can't move on after they lose a loved one. We let them say their goodbyes so they can.” He side-eyed Daisy. “But we ain’t a charity. A guy's gotta make a living.”

“And?” Daisy asked.

“And,” Frieda repeated. “When we see a few young girls, we know how to make them pay a bit more. When I say a few words in gibberish and add curse to it, I can guarantee in a few days someone will be back.”

“How?” Daisy asked.

“When you put the idea of a curse in someone's head, they start to believe in it,” Frieda explained. “Every time something goes wrong - they think curse. They add all the little things that go wrong in life up and start to believe it. When a pen bursts and ink gets everywhere - cursed. When the alarm doesn't go off and they are late - cursed. When the car won't start - cursed. They come back to see If I can help lift the curse.”

"And when they come back," Matt said, "they have to pay again. So what about the potion?"

"It was a few hard candies and some vodka." Freida explained, shrugging his shoulders. "Drink enough of it and you'll believe you are seeing the light."

"And the curse on me?" Daisy asked.

"Sorry, honey," Freida replied. "You two ain't special - unless you count being chumps. You paid ten times what other people do for that curse cure." He chuckled. "I'm still not giving it back, either. For what it's worth I would have let you say goodbye to your grandmother if you made another appointment. I was just milking it a bit for some extra bucks. It's coming up on the end of the month. I have bills to pay."

"It's fine," Matt replied. Knowing it or not, the psychic had done them a service. "Thanks for your time."

"Don't come back," Frieda yelled behind them. The sound of the baseball game returned.

The pressure of Matt's hand on her back ushered her onto the sidewalk. "Are you okay?"

"A bit confused," Daisy admitted.

"The concoction Frieda gave me wasn't real," Matt explained. "It acted as a placebo. I believed it was going to show me what I needed to see. In the end, it was my own abilities that I was tapping into."

So," Daisy replied, "Frieda really did help."

"Yes," Matt said. "But he doesn't know that. Without his help, I wouldn't have found a way to save you."

"Seems like a strange coincidence, doesn't it?" Daisy asked.

"Yeah," Matt admitted. "It does. I'm glad we decided to come back and thank them, or we never would have known the truth."

"I think we would have figured it out eventually. Do you smell that?" Daisy asked. "It's the same cigar scent I smelt last time we were here. Probably the same person."

"Most likely," Matt replied, glancing back at the psychic's home. Out of the corner of his eye, he caught a glimpse of a shadow as the front door closed.

"Is something wrong?" Daisy asked.

Matt pressed his lips together, the corners turning down. "Nope," he answered, making a popping noise on the end. "We should finish packing. I can't wait to show you your new home."

Chapter Nineteen

Matt opened the newspaper he'd grabbed before they left. He'd put off reading it after seeing the front page headline was about the doomsday clock ticking away. After what they had been through, he'd had enough of being a hero for a while.

He read two sentences and flipped the page, not wanting to ruin his jovial mood. Coffee splattered over the sides of his mug as it hit the table. He couldn't believe what he was reading. Fabulous Frieda and his assistant Maria had been found dead.

He folded the newspaper making it easier to read the one article. He scanned the information. The bodies were found in their home together with the murder weapon - a gun. He read further down. The gun was registered to Father Galen, whose whereabouts were currently unknown. It went on to mention the two missing priests and ask anyone with information to contact local police.

"Good morning," Daisy said, entering the kitchen. "Anything interesting in the paper?"

"Good morning," Matt replied, placing the newspaper face down on the table, just missing spilled coffee. "It's all rather depressing. I'll spare you the details."

"Have you been down to check on your new friends?" Daisy asked, pouring herself a cup of coffee.

"Not yet," Matt answered. "I wouldn't actually call them my friends."

"Uh-huh," Daisy said, rolling her eyes.

"I couldn't just leave them," Matt explained. "And it's a good thing I didn't. That ghost hunting crew broke into the lower levels only hours after the move. You don't mind them being here, do you? They don't come out much."

Daisy wrapped her arms around his neck from behind. "No, of course not. This place is way too big as it is. When you said we were going to live in your home, I had no idea it was a mansion like this. I doubt I'd ever get around to seeing the lower levels anyways."

"Lumpkin seems to be happy with the situation," Matt stated. "I have to admit I like the idea of having information at my fingertips." He wiggled his fingers in Daisy's direction.

"Have you found anything?" Daisy asked.

"Not yet," Matt admitted. "But don't worry. We have time. Something will come up." He rubbed her arm.

"I'm not sure there is a way to make a human immortal," Daisy replied. "You might have to accept I am going to grow old and die."

"I'm not giving up that easy," Matt said, watching her walk to the counter. "For now, don't touch any strange plants growing in the garden and you should probably stay up here."

"Why's that?" she asked, not wanting a reply. "Because you don't think I can handle a dwarf and a dragon?"

"No," Matt answered, chuckling. "Because I don't think a dwarf and a dragon can handle you. Although, I'm not quite sure Lumpkin is a dwarf."

"You could ask," Daisy suggested.

"That would make for an interesting conversation. I think I'll hold off on possibly insulting Lumpkin for now. He can get a bit grumpy."

"Unlike you, of course," Daisy joked.

"Of course." The smile on his face quickly changed to concern. A familiar chill on his spine told him they were about to have company. "We have a visitor," Matt announced. "Stay here for now. It's probably just someone looking for the records room. I thought I made the instructions clear enough to keep strangers away from the front."

He folded the newspaper under his arm and headed for the front door, opening it before the bell had a chance to ring.

"Matt."

"Frank. What are you doing here?"

"Checking up on you, of course," Frank answered. "Do you have a moment?"

Matt glanced at the angel's cigar. "Mind if we walk at the same time? She doesn't like smoke."

"I'd prefer it, actually." Frank replied.

"You haven't said exactly why you are here," Matt reminded the angel. His long legs easily took two steps at a time on the way down the front steps to the circular driveway.

"I did," Frank argued. "I'm here to check up on you. You may have broken the curse, but my employers feel they still have a vested interest in keeping tabs on you."

"Employers? Interesting choice of words." Matt laughed. "Why would they be interested in me?" he asked, leading the way around the grounds.

“Let me see,” Frank said, his eyes facing upwards and lips puckered. “You managed to break into a hidden stash of weapons; turned one of their best servants into dust, leaving behind only a gun; broke a curse; and now have some unusual house guests.”

“Does it matter who stays in my home?” Matt asked.

“It does if you were planning a rebellion,” Frank answered. “But we both know you aren't a hero. You wanted to save your woman, not start a revolution. You've done that. Nod your head and I can report the information back.”

Matt nodded. “I'm not sure a dragon and Lumpkin constitute a force big enough to take down Gods,” he commented. “What happens now?”

“Nothing, I expect,” Frank answered. “You go on with your life as if none of this ever happened. That reminds me. I have a gift for the little lady to deliver.”

Matt caught a stopwatch that had been lobbed in his direction. “From who?”

“Oddly enough, Death,” Frank answered, blowing out a ring of smoke.

“Why a stopwatch? Am I missing something?” Matt asked examining the piece. It looked rather ordinary for a gift.

“It is used to measure time,” Frank explained. “Think of Death as an accountant who needs to balance books. There can't be a deficit or a surplus. It throws everything out of whack and it has to be fixed. Of course, when it comes to the Grim Reaper, time is currency. Instead of dollars and cents, it's minutes and seconds.”

“I'm not sure I understand what this has to do with our situation,” Matt said.

“How many times has she died?” Frank asked.

“Thousands,” Matt replied. “I lost count a long time ago.”

“Well, Death didn't,” Frank stated. “Every time she died because of the curse, she was robbed of time she should have lived - precious moments that should have been hers. All that has been collecting - in there.” He pointed to the watch. “Death is returning it all to her... to set the books straight.” He twirled his hand in a circle, smoke from the cigar he was holding making rings. They collided into one cloud. He waved it away.

“So if she presses this button...”

“If she presses that button,” Frank interrupted, “she'll live a very long time. One might even go so far as call her an immortal.” He smiled, clenching the cigar between his teeth.

“I guess now I understand what the reaper meant saying the God's curses were messing up things.” Matt said. “Thank you.”

“It's from Death, not me,” Frank reminded. He walked over to a freshly planted garden bed. “Peach-coloured daisies,” he muttered with a half-chuckle. “Takes me back to my younger days. You know angels had a belief if you found one in the wild, it meant eternal happiness. It's been a while since I thought about that. I never thought I'd see them in someone's garden. Well, enough reminiscing. The Gods don't like to be kept waiting.”

“Will we see you again?” Matt asked.

“I hope not,” Frank replied. “Hopefully, you'll be left alone. Do me a favour - take care of her. Cherish the chance you've been given. And for goodness sakes make her an honest woman. Give her the white dress, the walk down the aisle and everything a bride could want.”

“I have every intention of marrying her,” Matt said, smiling. “Did you want an invitation?”

Frank shook his head. “Nope,” he answered. “My place isn't here. I'll be heading off.”

“To where?” Matt asked. “What happens to you? If I can break a curse...”

“Two very different curses,” Frank said. “I've accepted my fate. Besides, you aren't a hero - remember? That is what the Gods want to hear.”

Matt nodded.

Chapter Twenty

Matt loved to watch her. Here, in the middle of a field, she looked free and happy. Every twirl and step made his smile grow. She ran ahead chasing a butterfly.

"Look!" Daisy called out. "I don't believe it!"

Matt broke into a jog to catch up to her. "What did you find?" he asked.

"A wild peach-coloured daisy," she replied. "It's beautiful. I always thought it was a folktale."

He squatted beside her. "Pretty. Looks real to me," he said reaching forward.

She swatted his hand before he had a chance to pick it. "Don't! You'll ruin the chance someone else will find it. Just seeing it is enough for our eternal happiness."

Matt could hear the clicks of wheels turning in his head. How did he miss all the clues? He fell backwards into a sitting position on the ground. Everything became clear as he watched all the loose ends of the past few weeks tie themselves up in his thoughts.

Finding the two psychics and their death; the use of the priest's gun; the help of the Grim Reaper; Daisy's grandmother knowing about the weapons; it all pointed to one thing. Someone else was behind saving Daisy - someone who cared about her as much as he did.

Matt smiled. “We need to set a wedding date,” he blurted out. “I'd like to make an honest woman of you.” He had, after all, promised her father that he would.

Right now, whatever else the future held was a blank page. Perhaps one day he'd lead a rebellion to save all those who had been cursed. Until then, he'd keep Frank's secret as safe as Daisy herself.

Author's Message

I hope you enjoyed reading Matt and Daisy's story as much as I did writing it. Be sure to watch social media or my website for more Cursed by the Gods stories coming soon.

Thank you for reading! If you enjoyed this story, please browse through some on my other titles currently available.

ABOUT THE AUTHOR

C.A. King is the recipient of several awards, including: The Hamilton Spectator Readers' Choice Award for 2017 Best Author; The Brant News Readers' Choice Award for 2017 Best Author; Readers' Favourite award in the short story/novella category; the 2017 SIBA Award for Best New Adult; and the 2017 SIBA Award for Best Novella.

Currently residing in Brantford, Ontario Canada, she lives with her two sons. She began her writing career after the tragic loss of her parents and husband. Redirecting her emotions through writing became therapeutic in her battle with depression and in 2014 she decided to publish some of her works.

Other Titles from C.A. King

The Portal Prophecies

These great titles in C.A. King's The Portal Prophecies series are available now at most online book retailers:

A Keeper's Destiny

A Halloween's Curse

Frost Bitten

Sleeping Sands

Deadly Perceptions

Finding Balance

Volume I (Books 1-3)

Volume II (Books 4-6)

The prophecies are the key to their survival. Can they solve them in time?

Shattering the Effects of Time

Join the Shinning brothers, Jessie, Dezi and Pete as they set out on a quest to save their younger sister. No magic known to them or their friends has ever been able to reverse the grip of time. A few legends, however, exist mentioning ancient items that may hold the key to do exactly that.

This brand new series will take you on a search for the Fountain of Youth and Mermaids; a quest for the Holy Grail; a trip to visit Daryl the mountain guru, in the hunt for the Cinamani Stone; on a search for Ambrosia, the food of the Gods; and other adventures.

Surviving the Sins: Answering the Call

The prophecies are being rewritten. This time someone is using the seven deadly sins: Lust; Gluttony; Greed; Sloth; Wrath; Envy; and Pride, to unlock an ancient evil. The book falls into Jade's hands to answer destiny's call. Can she survive the sins?

Surviving the Sins: Pride

No one is safe when a witch's pride is at stake.

Prudance is back in Pewterclaw, and she isn't about to give up her prestigious status without a fight - especially not because of vampires. As an eighth-generation witch, she plans to do whatever it takes to stop the proposed new legislation from becoming law, including waking the dead for help.

Humility isn't in her vocabulary. With an ego spinning out of control and ancestral power at her fingertips, Prudance weaves a plot to keep Jade and Gavin separated. Will it be enough to satisfy the spirits she summoned?

When her pride costs more than she bargained for, someone has to pay the tab - but who will it be?

Surviving the Sins: Lust

What Mother doesn't know won't hurt her.

Lucinda has spent her entire existence running The Organization and looking after Mother's needs without complaint. That's about to change. A burning desire had manifested inside her - one she could no longer deny... Lust.

When Constable Safron Black shows up unexpected with news of an imprisoned God, Lucinda unravels. With power fuelling her passion, she'll do anything to make Morynx her mate.

****

Jade and her friends find themselves at a standstill. They have already failed to stop Pride from completing its task and they haven't located any victims for the other six sins. A strange fire in the municipal office puts them hot on the trail of what could be answers. Will they be in time to stop the dial from moving and further opening the way for Morynx?

When Leaves Fall: A Different Point of View Story

Ralph wakes up to what others only experience in a nightmare. Chained to a shed, he has no idea where he is, or who his captor is. His memories a blurred at best. As the days press on he finds himself experiencing a roller coaster of feelings. Hunger, thirst and pain become his only companions. Flashbacks of a happier time are all he has to keep him going. As his situation deteriorates, he finds himself doubting the very things he wants most - a family.

When Leaves Fall is a dramatic-thriller with a twist. Keep the tissue box close for the ending.

Tomoiya's Story

A Vampire Tale. She had a secret but she wasn't the only one who had something to hide.

Book I ~ Escape to Darkness

Book II ~ Collecting Tears

Book III~ Coming Soon

Flower Shields: A Four Horsemen Novel

Meet the four horsemen: Michael, Gabrielle, Uriel and Raphael. For centuries their job has been to guard the gates of hell, making sure they never open. Without the keys, there was never any real threat. That's about to change. There are rumours on the horizon that demon followers unearthed scrolls that explain exactly how to find the lost keys. This new battle is a race to see which side locates them first.

Michael couldn't care less about the love story behind how and why the world was created. In fact, nothing matters to him other than keeping the gates to hell closed. If one of the lost keys ever fell into the wrong hands, all humanity would be doomed. He's not going to let that happen - at any cost.

****

Tara's life is nothing short of a disaster. She's managed to flunk out of college with about the same amount of dignity as every relationship she's been in. The only constant in her life has been her love for flowers. When she's attacked at work, a stranger comes to her aid. Michael might be good-looking, but he's also arrogant, bossy and crazy. He's also her only chance to figure out who attacked her and why. Should she follow her heart and trust him - or listen to her head and run?

Drawing Strength From Words: A Four Horsemen Novel

Meet the four horsemen: Michael, Gabrielle, Uriel and Raphael.

For centuries their sole purpose has been guarding the sealed gates to hell. Without keys, there was never any real threat. That was about to change...

For Gabrielle, protecting mankind was merely a job for which she received little credit. The vast insecurities of men altered history itself, portraying her as a masculine brute. Taking a back seat to her brothers seemed the right thing to do, but left a bitter taste in her mouth and an impenetrable barricade shielding her heart.

****

Ryder bounced around the system from the moment both his parents were killed. Between that and run-ins with the law for crimes he never committed, it seemed the whole world was conspiring against him. Never growing attached to anyone was rule number one: a rule he'd never broken until a white-haired vixen, with blocks of ice on her shoulders, walked right into his life. Melting through those frosty layers became all that mattered, even if that meant sacrificing himself in the process.

Miracles Not Included

A heartfelt romantic story about: life; love; loss; and learning to love again. If only life came with instructions and a warning label ~ Miracles Not Included.

****

Chris was born to be a writer. Even the smallest of details couldn't pass without notice, often becoming part of a plot for her next novel. The one thing she never saw coming was her husband's sudden illness.

Jason loved his wife from the moment they met. Nothing could ever change that - nothing except the death sentence he'd been handed - a terminal cancer diagnosis.

His story was ending: Hers was starting a new chapter and more than one miracle was needed to turn the page.

Twisted Tales of a Dead End Street

A paranormal mystery laced with comedic undertones: Twisted Tales of a Dead End Street.

Nine neighbours were invited to the mysterious dinner party at 9 Nine Street. Their host, the owner of the mansion, had more planned for the evening than just roast beef. When the secret of their quiet street was revealed, everything changed, blurring the lines between the tangible and the paranormal.

Was the number nine the difference between life and death? Would any of them survive long enough to uncover the truth? They would each soon find out this wasn't a simple case of who-done-it so much as one of what was being done and by whom.

Shot Through The Heart: A Faerie Tale

A tale of two worlds - one filled with magic; the other void of it. But what happened to those trapped between the two? Adelia was about to find out...

Magic and structure were the foundations of her existence. Temptation controlled the ability to destroy everything she knew. The world of men held a powerful allure over her heart, waking that which had long been dormant. It enticed her, snagging her in a web of emotions.

A decision had to be made. Was feeling love for the first time worth sacrificing magic and immortality?

www.ingramcontent.com/pod-product-compliance
Ingram Content Group UK Ltd.
Pitfield, Milton Keynes, MK11 3LW, UK
UKHW041943190726
13854UKWH00004B/1770